DIRTY TALK

LAUREN LANDISH

Edited by
VALORIE CLIFTON
Edited by
STACI ETHERIDGE

DIRTY TALK

BY LAUREN LANDISH

He makes dirty sound so good. So right.

The moment I heard his velvety voice growl that I'm his 'Kitty Kat', I knew I was in trouble.

Derrick 'The Love Whisperer' King gives out relationship and sex advice on the radio to everyone, but he's giving me something a bit more personal. Nobody's ever talked to me the way he does. Daring, Demanding, Sexy... and oh so **Dirty**.

Maybe we started this whole thing a little backwards. Sex first and getting to know each other after. But as we get closer, he's healing the cracks in my untrusting heart and making me believe that maybe fairy tales do come true.

I feel beautiful and hopeful when he worships my body. I feel dirty and naughty when he whispers filthy things in my ear.

But is it real? Can something so bad **really** be good for me?

And more importantly, against all odds, can it last... **forever**?

Join my mailing list (www.laurenlandish.com) and receive 2 FREE ebooks! You'll also be the first to know of new releases, sales, and giveaways. If you're on Facebook, come join my Reader Group!

CHAPTER 1

KATRINA

"*C*heckmate, bitch," I exclaim as I do a victory dance that's comprised of fist pumps and ass wiggles in my chair while my best friend Elise laughs at me. I turn in my seat and start doing a little half-stepping Rockettes dance. "Can-can, I just kicked some can-can, I so am the wo-man, and I rule this place!"

Elise does a little finger dance herself, cheering along with me. "You go, girl. Winner, winner, chicken dinner. Now let's eat!"

I laugh with her, joyful in celebrating my new promotion at work, regardless of the dirty looks the snooty ladies at the next table are shooting our way. I get their looks. I mean, we are in the best restaurant in the city. While East Robinsville isn't New York or Miami, we're more of a Northeastern suburb of . . . well, everything in between. This just isn't the sort of restaurant where five-foot-two-inch women in work clothes go shaking their ass while chanting something akin to a high school cheer.

But right now, I give exactly zero fucks. "Damn right, we can eat! I'm the youngest person in the company to ever be promoted to Senior Developer and the first woman at that level. Glass ceiling? Boom, busting through! Boys' club? Infiltrated." I mime like I'm sneaking in, shoulders hunched and hands pressed tightly in front of me before splaying my arms wide with a huge grin. "Before they know it, I'm gonna have that boys' club watching chick flicks and the whole damn office is going to be painted pink!"

Elise snorts, shaking her head again. "I still don't have a fucking clue what you actually do, but even I understand the words *promotion* and *raise*. So huge congrats, honey."

She's right, no one really understands when I talk about my job. My brain has a tendency to talk in streams of binary zeroes and ones that make perfect sense to me, but not so much to the average person. When I was in high school, I even dreamed in Java.

And even I don't really understand what my promotion means. Senior Developer? Other than the fact that I get updated business cards with my fancy new title next week, I'm not sure what's changed. I'm still doing my own coding and my own work, just with a slightly higher pay grade. And when I say slightly, I mean barely a bump after taxes. Just enough for a bonus cocktail at a swanky club on Friday maybe. *Maybe* more at year end, they'd said. Ah, well, I'm excited anyway. It's a first step and an acknowledgement of my work.

The part people do get is when my company turns my

strings of code into apps that go viral. After my last app went number one, they were forced to give me a promotion or risk losing my skills to another development company. They might not understand the zeroes and ones, but everyone can grasp dollars and cents, and that's what my apps bring in.

I might be young at only twenty-six, and female, as evidenced by my long honey-blonde hair and curvy figure, but as much as I don't fit the stereotypical profile of a computer nerd, they had to respect that my brain creates things that no one else does. I think it's my female point of view that really helps. While a chunk of the other people in the programming field fit the stereotype of being slightly repressed geeks who are more comfortable watching animated 'girlfriends' than talking to an actual woman, I'm different. I understand that merely slapping a pink font on things or adding sparkly shit and giving more pre-loaded shopping options doesn't make technology more 'female-friendly.'

It's insulting, honestly. But it gives me an edge in that I know how to actually create apps that women like and want to use. Not just women, either, based on sales. I'm getting a lot of men downloading my apps too, especially men who aren't into tech-geeking out every damn thing they own.

And so I celebrate with Elise, holding up our glasses of wine and clinking them together in a toast. Elise sips her wine and nods in appreciation, making me glad we went with the waiter's recommendation. "So you're killing it on the job front. What else is going on? How are things with you and Kevin?"

Elise has been my best friend since we met at a college recruiting event. She's all knockout looks and sass, and I'm short, nervous, and shy in professional situations, but we clicked. She knows I've been through the wringer with some previous boyfriends, and even though Kevin is fine —well-mannered, ambitious, and treats me right—she just doesn't care for him for some reason. So my joyful buzz is instantly dulled, knowing that she doesn't like Kevin.

"He's fine," I reply, knowing it's not a great answer, but I also know she's going to roast me anyway. "He's been working a lot of hours so I haven't even seen him in a few days, but he texts me every morning and night. We're supposed to go out for dinner this weekend to celebrate."

Elise sighs, giving me that look that makes her normally very cute face look sort of like a sarcastic basset hound. "I'm glad, I guess. Not to beat a dead horse," —*too late*— "but you really can do better. Kevin is just so . . . meh. There's no spark, no fire between you two. It's like you're friends who fuck."

I duck my chin, not wanting her to read on my face the woeful lack of fucking that has been happening, but I'm too transparent.

"Wait . . . you two *do* fuck, right?" Elise asks, flabbergasted. "I figured that was why you were staying with him. I was sure he must be great in the sack or you'd have dumped his boring ass a long time ago."

I bite my lip, not wanting to get into this with her . . . again. But one of Elise's greatest strengths is also one of her most annoying traits as well. She's like a dog with a bone and isn't going to let this go.

"Look, he's fine," I finally reply, trying to figure out how much I need to feed Elise before she gives me a measure of peace. "He's handsome, treats me well, and when we have sex, it's good . . . I guess. I don't believe in some Prince Charming who is going to sweep me off my feet to a castle where we'll have romantic candlelit dinners, brilliant conversation, and bed-breaking sexcapades. I just want someone to share the good and bad times with, some companionship."

Elise holds back as long as she can before she explodes, her snort and guffaw of derision getting even more looks in our direction. "Then get a fucking Golden Retriever and a rabbit. The buzzing kind that uses rechargeable batteries."

One of the ladies at the next table huffs, seemingly aghast at Elise's outburst, and they stand to move toward the bar on the other side of the restaurant, far away from us. "Well, if this is the sort of trash that passes for dinner conversation," the older one says as she sticks her nose far enough into the air I wonder if it's going to be clipped by the ceiling fans, "no wonder the country's going to hell under these Millennials!"

She storms off before Elise or I can respond, but the second lady pauses slightly and talks out of the side of her mouth. "Sweetie, you do deserve more than *fine*."

With a wink, she scurries off after her friend, leaving behind a grinning Elise. "See? Even snooty old biddies know that you deserve more than *meh*."

"I know. We've had this conversation on more than one occasion, so can we drop it?" I plead between clenched teeth before calming slightly. "I want to celebrate and catch up, not argue about my love life."

Always needing the last word, Elise drops her voice, muttering under her breath. "What love life?"

"That's low."

Elise holds her hands up, and I know I've at least gotten a temporary reprieve. "Okay then, if we're sticking to work, I got a new scoop that I'm running with. I'm writing a piece about a certain famous someone who got caught sending dick pics to a social media princess. Don't ask me who because I can't divulge that yet. But it'll be all there in black and white by next week's column."

Elise is an investigative journalist, a rather fantastic one whose talents are largely being wasted on celebrity news gossip for the tabloid paper she writes for. I can't even call it a paper, really. With the downfall of actual print news, most of her stuff ends up in cyberspace, where it's digested, Tweeted, hashtagged, and churned out for the two-minute attention span types to gloat over for a moment before they move on to . . . well, whatever the next sound bite happens to be.

Every once in awhile, she'll get to do something much more newsworthy, but mostly it's fact-checking and ass-covering before the paper publishes stories celebrities would rather see disappear. I know what burns her ass even more is when she has to cover the stories where some downward-trending celebrity manufactures a scandal just to get some social media buzz going before their latest attempt at rejuvenating a career that peaked about five years ago.

This one at least sounds halfway interesting, and frankly, better than my love life, so I laugh. "Why would he send a dick pic to someone on social media? Wouldn't he assume she'd post it? What a dumbass!"

"No, it's usually close-ups and they're posted anonymously," Elise says with a snort. "Of course, she knows because she sees the user name on their direct message, but she cuts it out so that it's posted to her page as an anonymous flash of flesh. Look."

She pulls out her phone, clicking around to open an app, one I didn't design but damn sure wish I had. It's got one hell of a sweet interface, and Elise is using it to organize her web pages better than anything the normal apps have. It takes Elise only a moment to find the page she wants.

"See?" she says, showing me her phone. "People send her messages with dick pics, tit pics, whatever. If she deems them sexy enough, she posts them with little blurbs and people can comment. She also does Q-and-As with followers, shows faceless pics of herself, and gives little shows sometimes. Kinda like porn but more 'real people' instead of silicone-stuffed, pump-sucked, fake moan scenes."

She scrolls through, showing me one image after another

of body part close-ups. Some of them . . . well damn, I gotta say that while they might not be professionals or anything, it's a hell of a lot hotter than anything I'm getting right now. "Wow. That's uhh . . . quite something. I don't get it, but I guess lots of folks are into it. Wait."

She stops scrolling at my near-shout, smirking. "What? See something you like?"

My mouth feels dry and my voice papery. "Go back up a couple."

She scrolls back up and I read the blurb above a collage of pics. *Little titty fuck with my new boy toy today. Look at my hungry tits and his thick cock. After this, things got a little deeper, if you know what I mean. Sorry, no pics of that, but I'll just say that he was insatiable and I definitely had a very good morning. ;)*

The pictures show a close-up of her full cleavage, a guy's dick from above, and then a few pictures of him stroking in and out of her pressed-together breasts. I'm not afraid to say the girl's got a nice rack that would probably have most of my co-workers drooling and the blood rushing from their brains to their dicks, but that's not what's causing my stomach to drop through the floor.

I know that dick.

It's the same, thick with a little curve to the right, and I can even see a sort of donut-shaped mole high on the man's thigh, right above the shaved area above the base of his cock.

Yes, that mole seals it.

That's Kevin.

His cock with another woman, fucking her for social media, thinking I'd probably never even know. He has barely touched me lately, but he's willing to do it almost publicly with some social media slut?

I realize Elise is staring at me, her previous good-natured look long gone to be replaced by an expression of concern. "Kat, are you okay? You look pale."

I point at her phone, trying my best to keep my voice level. "That post? The one right there?"

"Oh, Titty Fuck Girl?" Elise asks. "She's on here at least once a month with a new set of pics. Apparently, she loves her rack. I still think they're fake. Why?"

"She's talking about Kevin. That's him."

She gasps, turning the phone to look closer. "Holy shit, honey. Are you sure?"

I nod, tears already pooling in my eyes. "I'm sure."

She puts her phone down on the table and comes around the table to hug me. "Shit. Shit. Shit. I am so sorry. I told you that douchebag doesn't deserve someone like you. You're too fucking good for him."

I sniffle, nodding, but deep inside, I know that this is always how it goes. Every single boyfriend I've ever had ended up cheating on me. I've tried playing hard to get. I've tried being the good little go-along girlfriend. I've even tried being myself, which seems to be somewhere in between, once I figured out who I actually was.

It's even worse in bed, where I've tried being vanilla, being aggressive, and being submissive. And again, being myself, somewhere in the middle, when I figured out what I enjoyed from the experimentation.

But honestly, I've never been satisfied. No matter what, I just can't seem to find that 'sweet spot' that makes me happy and fulfilled in a relationship. And while I've tried everything, depending on the guy, it never works out. The boyfriends I've had, while few in number considering I can count them on one hand, all eventually cheated, saying that they just wanted something different. Something that's *not* me.

Apparently, Kevin's no different. My mood shifts wildly from self-pity to anger to finally, a numb acceptance. "What a fucking jerk. I hope he likes being a boy toy for a social media slut, because he's damn sure not my boyfriend anymore."

"That's the spirit," Elise says, refilling my wine glass. "Now, how about you and I finish off this bottle, get another, and by the time you're done, you'll have forgotten all about that loser while we take a cab back to your place?"

"Maybe I will just get a dog, and I sure as hell already have a buzzing rabbit. Several of them, in fact," I mutter. "You know what? They're better than he ever was by a damn country mile."

"Rabbits . . . they just keep going and going and going," Elise jokes, trying to keep me in good spirits. She twirls her hands in the air like the famous commercial bunny and signals for another bottle of wine.

She's right. Fuck Kevin.

CHAPTER 2

*M*y black leather office chair creaks, an annoying little trend it's developed over the past six months that's the primary reason I don't use it in the studio. Admittedly, that's probably for the better because if I had a chair this comfortable in the studio, I'd be too relaxed to really be on point for my shows. Still, it's helpful to have something nice like this office since it's a hell of a big step up from the days when my office was also the station's break room. "All right, hit me. What's on the agenda for today's show?"

My co-star, Susannah, checks her papers, making little checkmarks as she goes through each item. She's an incessant checkmarker, and I have no idea how the fuck she can read her sheets by the end of the day. "The overall theme for today is cheaters, and I've got several emails pulled for that so we can stay on track. We'll field calls, of course, and some will be on topic and some off, like always. I'll try and screen them as best I can, and we should be all set."

I nod, trying to mentally prep myself for another three-hour stint behind the mic, offering music, advice, hope, and sometimes a swift kick in the pants to our listeners. Two years ago, I never would've believed that I'd be known as the 'Love Whisperer' on a radio talk segment called the same thing. Part Howard Stern, part Dr. Phil, part DJ Love Below, I've found a niche that's just . . . unique.

I started out many years ago as a jock, playing football on my high school team with dreams of college ball. A seemingly short derailment after an injury led me to do sports reporting for my high school's news and I fell in love.

After that, my scholarships to play football never came, but it didn't bother me as much as I thought it would. I decided to chase after a sports broadcast degree instead, marrying my passion for football and my love of reporting.

I spent four years after graduation doing daily sports talks from three to six as the afternoon drive-home DJ. It wasn't a big station, just one of the half-dozen stations that existed as an alternative for people who didn't want to listen to corporate pop, hip-hop, or country. It was there I received that fateful call.

Looking back, it's kind of crazy, but a guy had called in bitching and moaning about his wife not understanding his need to follow all these wild superstitions to help his team win.

"I'm telling you D, I went to church and asked God himself. I said, if you can bless the Bandits with a win, I'll show myself true and wear those ugly ass socks my pastor gave me for Christmas the year before and never wash them again. You know what happened?"

Of course, everyone could figure out what happened. Still, I respectfully told him that I didn't think his unwashed socks were doing a damn thing for his beloved team on the basketball court, but if he didn't put those fuckers in the washing machine, they were sure going to land him in divorce court.

He sighed and eventually gave in when I told him to wash the socks, thank his wife for putting up with his shit, and full-out romance her to bed and do his damndest to make up for his selfish ways.

And that was that. A new show and a new me were born. After a few marketing tweaks, I've been the so-called 'Love Whisperer' for almost a year now, helping people who ask for advice to get the happily ever after they want.

Ironically, I'm single. Funny how that works out, but all the good advice I try to give stems from my parents who were happily married for over forty years before my mom passed. I won't settle for less than the real thing, and I try to advise my listeners to do the same.

And then there's the sex aspect of my job.

Talking about relationships obviously involves discussing sex with people, as that's one of the major areas that cause problems for folks. At first, talking about all the crazy shit people want to do even made me blush a little, but eventually, it's just gotten to be second nature.

Want to talk about how to get your wife to massage your prostate? Can do. Want to talk about how your girlfriend wants you to wear Underoos and call her Mommy? Can do. Want to talk about your husband never washing the dishes, and how you can get him to help? I can do that too.

All-in-one, real relationships at your service. Live from six to nine, five days a week, or available for download on various podcast sites and clip shows on the weekends. Hell of a lot for a guy who figured *making it* would involve becoming the voice of some college football team.

So I want to do a good job. And that means working well with Susannah, who is the control-freak yin to my laissez-faire yang. "Thanks. I know this week's topics from our show planning meeting, but I spaced on tonight's focus."

Susannah nods, unflappable. "No problem. Do you want to scan the emails or just do your thing?"

I smile at her. She already knows the answer. "Same as always, spontaneous. You know that even though I was a Boy Scout, being prepared for this doesn't do us any favors. I sound robotic when I read ahead. First read, real reactions work better and give the listeners knee-jerk common sense."

She shrugs, scribbling on her papers. "I know, just checking."

It's probably one of the reasons we work so well together, our totally different approaches to the show. Joining me from day one, she's the one who keeps our show running behind the scenes and keeps me on track on-air, serving as both producer and co-host. Luckily, her almost anal-retentive penchant for prep totally doesn't come across on the air, where she's the playful, comedic counter to my gruff, tell-it-like-it-is style.

"Then let's rock," I tell her. "Got your drinks ready?"

Susannah nods as we head toward the studio. Settling into my broadcast chair, a much less comfortable but totally silent one, I survey my normal spread of one water, one coffee, and one green tea, one for every hour we're gonna be on the air. With the top of the hour news breaks and spaced out music jams, I've gotten used to using the exactly four minute and thirty second breaks to run next door and drain my bladder if I need to.

Everything ready, we smile and settle in for another show. "Gooooood evening! It's your favorite 'Love Whisperer,' Derrick King here with my lovely assistant, Miss Susannah Jameson. We're ready for an evening of love, sex, betrayal, and lust, if you're willing to share. Our focus tonight is on cheaters and cheating. Are you being cheated on? Maybe *you* are the cheater? Call in and we'll talk."

The red glow from the holding calls is instant, but I traditionally go to an email first so that I can roll right in. "While Susannah is grabbing our first caller, I'll start with an email. Here's one from P. 'Dear Love Whisperer,' it says, 'my husband travels extensively for work, leaving me

17

home and so lonely. I don't know if he's cheating while he's gone, but I always wonder. I've started to develop feelings for my personal trainer, and I think I'm falling in love with him. What should I do?' "

I *tsk-tsk* into the microphone, making my displeasure clear. "Well, P, first things first. Your marriage is your priority because you made a vow. For better or worse, remember? It's simple. Talk to your husband. Maybe he's cheating, maybe he isn't. Maybe he's working his ass off so his bored wife can even *have* a trainer and you're looking for excuses to justify your own bad behavior. But talking to him is your first step. You need to explain your feelings and that you need him more than perhaps you need the money. Second, you need to get a life beyond your husband and trainer. I get the sense you need some attention and your trainer is giving it to you, so you think you're in love with him. Newsflash—he's being paid to give you attention. By your husband, it sounds like. That's not a healthy foundation for a relationship even if he is your soulmate, which I doubt."

I sigh and lower my voice a little. I don't want to cut this woman's guts out. I want to help her. "P, let's be honest. A good trainer is going to be personable. They're in a sales profession. They're not going to make it in the industry without either being the best in the world at what they do or having a good personality. And a lot of them have good bodies. Their bodies are their business cards. So it's natural to feel some attraction to your trainer. But that doesn't mean he's going to stick by you. Here's a challenge —tell your trainer you can't pay him for the next three months and see how available he is to just give you his time."

Susannah snickers and hits her mic button. "That's why I do group yoga classes. Only thing that happens there is sweaty tantric orgies. Ohmm . . . my . . ." Her initial yoga-esque ohm dissolves into a pleasure-induced moan that she fakes exceedingly well.

I roll my eyes, knowing that she does nothing of the sort. "To the point, though, fire your trainer because of your weakness and tell him why. He's a pro. He needs to know that his services were not the reason you're leaving. Next, get a hobby that fulfills you beyond a man and talk to your husband."

I click a button and a sound effect of a cheering audience plays through my headset. It goes on like this for a while, call after call, email after email of helping people.

Well, I hope I'm helping them. They seem to think I am, and I'm certainly giving it my best shot. In between, I mix in music and a hodgepodge of stuff that fits the daily themes. Tonight I've got some Taylor Swift, a little Carrie Underwood, some old-school TLC. I even, as a joke, worked in Bobby Brown at Susannah's insistence.

Coming back from that last one, I see Susannah gesture from her mini-booth and give the airspace over to her, letting her introduce the next caller. "Okay, Susannah's giving me the big foam finger, so what've we got?"

"You wish I had a big finger for you," Susannah teases like she always does on air—it's part of our act. "The next caller would like to discuss some rather incriminating photos she's come across. Apparently, Mr. Right was Mr. Everybody?"

I click the button, taking the call live on-air. "This is the 'Love Whisperer', who am I speaking with?"

The caller stutters, obviously nervous, and in my mind I know I have to treat this one gently. Some of the callers just want to laugh, maybe have their fifteen seconds of fame or get their pound of proverbial flesh by exposing their partner's misdeeds. But there are also callers like this, who I suspect really needs help. "This is Katrina . . . Kat."

Whoa, a first name. And from the sound of it, a real one. She's not making a thing up. I need to lighten the mood a little, or else she's gonna clam up and freak out on me. "Hello, Kitty Kat. What seems to be the problem today?"

I hear her sigh, and it touches me for some reason. "Well . . . I can't believe I actually got through, first of all. I worked up the nerve to dial the numbers but didn't expect an answer. I'm just . . . I don't even know what I am. I'm just a little lost and in need of some advice, I guess." She huffs out a humorless laugh.

I can hear the pain in her voice, mixed with nerves. "Advice? That I can do. That's what I'm here for, in fact. What's going on, Kat?"

"It's my boyfriend, or my soon-to-be ex-boyfriend, I guess. I found out today that he slept with someone else." She sounds like she's found a bit of steel as she speaks this time, and it makes her previous vulnerability all the more touching.

"Ouch," I say, truly wincing at the fresh wound. A day of cheat call? I'm sure the advertisers are rubbing their hands in glee, but I'm feeling for this girl. "I'm so sorry. I know that hurts and it's wrong no matter what. I heard something about compromising pics. Please tell me he didn't send you pics of him screwing someone else?"

She laughs but it's not in humor. "No, I guess that would've been worse, but he had sex with someone kind of Internet famous and she posted faceless pics of them together. But I recognized his . . . uhm . . . his . . ."

Let's just get the schlong out in the open, why don't we? "You recognized his penis? Is that the word you're looking for?"

"Yeah, I guess so," Kat says, her voice cutting through the gap created by the phone line. "He has a mole, so I know it's him."

There's something about her voice, all sweet and breathy that stirs me inside like I rarely have happen. It's not just her tone, either. She's in pain, but she's mad as fuck too, and I want to help her, protect her. She seems innocent, and something deep inside me wants to make her a little bit dirty.

"Okay, first, repeat after me. Penis, dick, cock." I wait, unsure if she'll do it but holding my breath in the hopes that she will.

"Uh, what?"

I feel a small smile come to my lips, and it's my turn to be a little playful. "Penis, dick, cock. Trust me, this is important for you. You can do it, Kitty Kat."

I hear her intake of breath, but she does what I demanded, more clearly than the shyness I expected. "Penis, dick, cock."

"Good girl," I growl into the mic, and through the window connecting our booths, I can see Susannah giving me a raised eyebrow. "Now say . . . I recognized his cock fucking her."

I say a silent prayer of thanks that my radio show is on satellite. I can say whatever I want and the FCC doesn't care.

I can tell Kat is with me now, and her voice is stronger, still sexy as fuck but without the lost kitten loneliness to it. "I recognized his cock fucking her tits."

My own cock twitches a little, and I lean in, smirking. "Ah, so the plot thickens. So Kat, how does it feel to say that?"

She sighs, pulling me back a little. "The words don't bother me. I'm just not used to being on the radio. But saying that about my boyfriend pisses me off. I can't believe he'd do that."

"So, what do you think you should do about it?" I ask, leaning back in my chair and pulling my mic toward me. "Is this a 'talk it through and our relationship will be stronger on the other side of this' type situation, or is this a 'hit the road, motherfucker, and take Miss Slippy-Grippy Tits with you?' Do you want my opinion or do you already know?"

"You're right," Kat says, chuckling and sounding stronger again. "I already know I'm done. He's been a wham-bam-doesn't even say thank you, ma'am guy all along, and I've been hanging on because I didn't think I deserved better. But I don't deserve this. I'm better off alone."

Whoa, now, only half right there, Kat with the sexy voice. "You don't deserve this. You should have someone who treats you so well you never question their love, their commitment to you. Everyone deserves that. Hey, Kitty Kat? One more thing. Can you say 'cock' for me one more time? Just for ... entertainment."

I'm pushing the line here, both for her and for the show, but I ask her to do it anyway because I want, no need, to hear her say it.

She laughs, her voice lighter even as I know the serious conversation had to hurt. "Of course, Love Whisperer. Anything for you. You ready? Cock." She draws the word out, the k a bit harsher, and I can hear the sass, almost an invitation, as she speaks.

"Ooh, thanks so much, Kitty Kat. Hold on the line just a second." My cock is now fully hard in my pants, and I'm not sure if my upcoming bathroom break is going to be to piss or to take care of that.

I click some buttons, sending the show to a song, Shaggy's

It Wasn't Me coming over the airwaves to keep the cheating theme rolling. "Susannah?"

"Yeah?"

"Handle the next call or so after the commercial break," I tell her. "Pick something . . . funny after that one."

"Gotcha," Susannah says, and I'm glad she's able to handle things like that. It's part of our system too that when I get a call that needs more than on-air can handle, she fills the gap. Usually with less serious questions or listener stories that always make for great laughs.

Checking my board, I click the line back, glad that Susannah can't hear me now. "Kat? You still there?"

"Yes?" she says, and I feel another little thrill go down my cock just at her word. God, this woman's got a sexy voice, soft and sweet with a little undercurrent of sassiness . . . or maybe I really, really need to get laid.

"Hey, it's Derrick. I just wanted to say thanks for being such a good sport with all of that."

"No problem," she says as I make a picture in my head of her. I can't fill in the details, but I definitely want to. "Thanks for helping me realize I need to walk away. I already knew it, but some inspiration never hurts."

"I really would like to hear the rest of the story if you don't mind calling me back. I want to hear how he grovels when he finds out what he's lost. Would you call me?"

I don't know what I'm doing. This is so not like me. I never talk to the callers after they're on air unless I think they're going to hurt themselves or others, and I certainly never invite them to call back. But something about her voice calls to me like a siren. I just hope she's not pulling me into the rocky shore to crash.

"You mean the show?" Kat asks, uncertain and confused. "Like . . . I dunno, like a guest or something?"

"Well, probably not, to be honest," I reply, crossing my fingers even as my cock says I need to take this risk. "We'll be done with the cheating theme tonight and it probably won't come back up for a couple of weeks. I meant . . . call me. I want to make sure you're okay afterward and standing strong."

"Okay."

Before she can take it back, I rattle off my personal cell number to her, half of my brain telling me this is brilliant and the other half saying it's the stupidest thing I've ever done. I might not have the FCC looking over my shoulder, but the satellite network is and my advertisers for damn sure are. Still . . . "Got it?"

"I've got it," Kat says. "I'll get back to you after I break up with Kevin. It's been a weird night and I guess it's going to get even weirder. Guess I gotta go tell Kevin his dick busted him on the internet and he can get fucked elsewhere . . . permanently. I can do this."

"Damn right, you can," I tell her. "You can do this, Kitty Kat. Remember, you deserve better. I'll be waiting for your report."

Kat laughs and we hang up. I don't know what just

happened but my body feels light, bubbly inside as I take a big breath to get ready for the next segment of tonight's show.

CHAPTER 3

KAT

I knock on the door to Kevin's apartment, the voice of Derrick the Love Whisperer still running around in my head. I deserve better than to be cheated on.

"Hey, babe," Kevin says when he opens his door. He's still wearing his 'work clothes,' a black tank top with *KH Nutrition* emblazoned on it along with track pants that are just a little tight and normally worn just a little low on his hips when he works out. I've never really understood why he does it, but it's part of his 'thang.' Every Instagram pic and video he does, he whips off the tank, adjusts his track pants in a way that highlights the Adonis belt V-cut of his abs, then flexes and sort of makes a hooting grunt before finishing the show with "KH, Bay-bay!"

I used to think it was sexy, in a musclehead, caveman-ish sort of way. No longer. "Don't 'hey, babe' me," I growl, looking up into his eyes. I'm not in work clothes, so I'm missing the extra inches of height my heels normally give me. But I'm a legit five-two of fury right now, so I don't care if he's nearly a foot taller. "How long have you been fucking her behind my back?"

"Huh?" Kevin asks, but in his eyes I can see he has a damn good idea what I'm talking about.

"Don't act stupid, you son of a bitch!" I hiss, poking him in the chest. "You know exactly what I'm talking about. Titty Fuck Girl. Where'd you meet her, the gym? When you went out shopping for a new smartphone with the money I gave you because you swore you needed the better camera for your Instagram page? How long has it been going on, Kevin?"

Kevin looks up and down the hallway. For a guy whose Internet presence makes him look like a big baller, he's living in a cracker box POS apartment building, and I know he's worried about his neighbors hearing me blab his private business. "Come on inside. We can talk—"

"If you don't tell me how long it's been going on, I'm going to put my knee right in your nuts," I growl. "This isn't a negotiation, Kevin." It really doesn't matter at this point. It's most likely just going to make me angrier, but I can't stop myself.

He looks like he's about to run but sighs. "Fine. I met her a couple of months ago when she came into the gym. I was filming a squat."

"What? So she just walked up behind you to compliment your form and suddenly, you're in bed?" I laugh, realizing just how short I sold myself. He's fake—the tan, the persona, the entire image. Just to get more followers.

Kevin looks sheepish but nods. "She said she'd promote my supps, do some spots on her Instagram feed, and let me shoot some selfies with her wearing a KH tank top."

"So you titty fucked her?" I hiss, shaking my head. Seriously, what the fuck? I can hardly take it as I stare at his chiseled face, wanting so badly to slap him. "Do you realize how ridiculous you sound right now? How stupid do you think I am?"

Kevin looks pouty, the same look he used when he hit me up for four hundred bucks for his new smartphone. "You never believe in me, never think I can be successful even though I work so hard."

It's in this moment that I see it. Though his face is schooled into a puppy dog look, his eyes are alight as he turns the blame back on me, thinking he's pulled one over on me once again. And all the fire leaves me. I'm mad he cheated, but I don't even really like him right now, and honestly, I haven't for a long time but was too afraid to do anything about it.

My voice takes a parental, lecturing tone. "You're not working. You're a lazy ass who spends hours at the gym bullshitting with the bros and thinking some scam is going to magically make you money without your having to actually do anything. But you know what? I looked the other way for too long even though everyone told me you were no good. None of that even matters now. You cheated on me. Done. Game over."

Kevin inhales, trying to stand at his tallest, most imposing. His forearms clench and his biceps start to strain as he puffs up. It strikes me that once upon a time, he'd stand over me like this and I'd find it so damn sexy I'd be instantly wet, but now, his attempt at intimidating me is just ridiculous. "You'll be sorry. You'll never find someone who treats you like I do, who satisfies you like I do."

God, how could I have been so blind? "Like you do? You know, I hope you're right because you treat me like an afterthought, using me as an ATM when you're a little short, screwing around, and blaming me for your lack of success when it's your own fault," I reply, keeping my voice calm but firm, not letting him get an inch on me. I'm not going to raise my voice, to yell or let him think that he's gotten to me, because for some reason, honestly, he hasn't. "And as for satisfied in bed, I have literally never had a single orgasm with you. Ever. I'm not gonna lie, your dick is nice to look at and photographs well, apparently, but you don't even know what to do with it. Sticking it in and out for two minutes before blowing into a condom and then rolling over to gasp while staring at the ceiling doesn't quite cut it, Kev. So yeah, I hope I never find someone who treats me like you do. I thought I could settle for content, just float along and not rock the boat, but I deserve so much more."

Before Kevin can reply, I turn and walk toward the stairs, not wanting to lose my nerve in front of him. It's not until I'm halfway down that the shakes start as the adrenaline leaves me, but I keep it cool until I get to my car.

One Week Later

A week since the blow-up with Kevin and I'm surprisingly not upset. Disappointed, sure, but if you end a one-year relationship with someone, shouldn't you feel sad? I've felt a lot of other emotions, anger mostly, but they've faded too. Instead, I'm just left with this . . . I guess more than anything, lack of things to do. I've got more free time on my hands, but I'm not sad or upset.

I guess the lack of depression goes to show how far apart we'd drifted and how unattached I was from him without even realizing it. Really, the most annoying part of this whole thing has been that I've had to change my gym membership because I didn't want drama or to limit myself to when I could or couldn't go based on his haunting the place.

Maybe I never really was in love with him. We'd met at the gym, and he'd been charming and admittedly hot, so when he asked me out, I said yes. Our dating just naturally progressed, and somewhere along the way, we started calling it a relationship, but who knows if he was ever really committed? I was faithful, but that was more out of habit and the fact that I would never cheat than any obvious commitment we had. It's not like he ever put a ring on it.

Even though it had been over a month since we'd been intimate, I'd gone to the doctor for a checkup just to be safe, and luckily, everything was clear. I can't believe he'd put me at risk, but I guess I should've seen it coming considering guys always cheat.

Taking the opportunity to do a purge on everything in my life, I've got the radio turned up and I'm cleaning my apartment like a mad woman when I hear the voice. *His* voice.

It's like velvet-covered gravel, and just a few words make me breathless and hot. "Good evening, listeners. Derrick King here, aka the 'Love Whisperer'. What's happening in your love life? Our focus tonight is on pushing boundaries in the bedroom. What's encouraging and fun? What's demanding and over the line? Call in if you've got something to discuss."

I've gone stock-still, my cleaning completely forgotten as his voice washes over me. I turn it up a little more as I finish sweeping, deciding everything else can wait as I listen.

Over the next few hours, Derrick is surprisingly simple in his answers to callers, who want to try a variety of things sexually but for whatever reason haven't discussed it with their partners. It's almost comical how every call gets into a groove, and it sort of goes like this:

I want to do this crazy thing.

Have you asked your partner?

No.

Talk to them. Maybe they're into it.

But I'm not sure they want to.

How could you know if you don't talk with them? If they are, great. If not, decide if it's a deal breaker and move forward according to your answer. Chances are it's not a deal-breaker if you're not doing it now.

It's funny and spiced up with plenty of little anecdotes and witticisms that leave me grinning, while his voice turns me on even as I'm comforted. I listen to his no-nonsense approach as he advocates conversation and honesty at every turn, and I only wish I had a man like that who'd actually talk and be honest with me.

As the show wraps up, I remember his request for me to call him back and tell him what happened with Kevin. He was probably just being nice and doesn't actually expect me to call, but something about it felt real.

I wait for a bit after the show ends to give him time to get out of the studio and wherever it is he goes after work, and then I call. I'm heading out anyway. I've got a late-night rumbling tummy that can only be satisfied by something cheesy and takeout.

The phone rings several times and I'm about to hang up, mad at myself for being stupidly excited about talking to *The Love Whisperer* again, when he answers.

"Talk to me."

It's the same purring growl. That panty-melting voice of his isn't an act.

"Hey, Love Whisperer. It's your Kitty Kat."

There's a throaty chuckle on the other end, but there's concern in it too, which helps me feel better. "*My* Kitty Kat now?" he asks, and I can hear the smile in his voice. "After a week went by, I wasn't sure if I was going to get that return call. I was starting to doubt whether I had an effect at all."

"You set me straight. Hold on. Let me put you on speaker. I've got this technogeek wonder phone that I love to use speaker on."

"Well, I'm in my office, so this isn't private . . . but tell me, how'd it go?"

I plug my phone into the charging dock in my dash and slip my Bluetooth earpiece in as I fire up my car. "First off, I can't believe I didn't listen to anyone."

Derrick

"I can't believe you're the type to settle for anyone," I reply, relaxing back in my office chair. It's late. Almost nobody is around the studio right now. It's one of the benefits of satellite radio, I guess. You can run a lot more shows pre-recorded. "So he fessed up?"

"He gave me the most ridiculous line of shit ever," Kat says, her breathy voice causing a stir in my pants. What the fuck is wrong with me? "He said that he did it because she was willing to pimp his line of supplements on her Instagram page."

"You're shitting me," I say, rolling my eyes. "What a stupid asshole."

"You're right there. Honestly, I waited a week to call because I wanted to get a clear head."

"I can understand that. So he fed you a line of bullshit, and you chucked his ass out on the street. That's what I wanted to hear."

"Not quite," Kat says. "I went to his apartment to give him the news. No waiting around."

"Good for you," I tell her. "So, that's it? I mean, I like it, but sounds a bit easy, don't you think?"

"Well, he did try to puff his chest out and tell me no man would ever treat me like he did or satisfy me like him. I took a little delight in telling him that I sure as hell hoped not since he's a cheater whom I had to fake it with because he'd never even made me . . ." Kat says with spunkiness before stopping herself short. "Uhm, I mean—"

"Wait, seriously?" I ask in a sputtering laugh. "Is that true? You weren't just busting his balls? Damn, Kat . . . for how long?"

"It's okay," she says, seemingly comfortable talking to me. "My best friend told me to get a dog or a new rabbit. Or both. She's probably right."

"A rabbit?" I ask, my brain half-buzzed from her voice. Fuck me, I need to get laid.

"Well, um, not a bunny rabbit," she replies, her voice becoming even a little breathier. "You know . . . a rabbit."

She makes a buzzing sound, and all of a sudden, it hits me. She's making me seem like an amateur. I talk about sex for a living. I shouldn't be caught off guard like this. Trying to maintain at least a veneer of professionalism, I clear my throat. "Yeah, I can see where that'd come in handy. Take matters into your own hands, so to speak. I've done that myself more than a few times."

What I just said sinks in for both of us, and the tension between us can be felt even over the phone lines. If I could see her right now, I'd swear we'd just crossed a line. And I'd probably see how far I could push to make a move.

Kat can feel it too. "So, uh, yeah, anyway. That was probably an overshare on my part. Sorry about that."

Fuck it. I don't know why I'm doing this, but I'm just gonna go for it. Her sweet voice is doing something magically delicious to me, something about her intriguing me in a way I haven't felt in a long while. Time to jump in the pool and see if she's willing to swim with me. I look around the studio, not seeing Susannah. "Not an overshare at all. I'm just in the middle of picturing you with your new pet bunny, what you would look like spread wide open with your tits pearled up, pussy pulsing around a little toy that can't fill it, and what you'd sound like when you come."

I know my voice has gotten deeper, lust making it even rougher than my usual smooth radio sound, but I can't stop it. I adjust myself in my jeans, glad she can't see the effect she's having on me right now.

There's a slight hitch in her voice as she adjusts to what I just said. "Derrick, wow. I don't know what to say to that. Fuck."

She's all but whispering by the end of her sentence and I wonder if she's touching herself to let out some tension. I don't even know what she looks like, but I don't care. I want to see her just like I said, maybe in a little skirt that's hiked up so she can show me as I inhale her scent. "You don't have to say anything unless you want me to stop."

I pause, hoping she doesn't say stop because I damn sure don't want to. I barely know this woman, this voice coming through my phone, but she's got me rock hard and on the edge with barely a word. I reach down and undo the button on my jeans, giving myself at least a little room to breathe.

"I think I need to—"

I interrupt, hoping to give her what she wants and needing my own release as well. "What do you need, Kitty Kat? I'll give it to you."

Kat pauses, and I can feel her trembling on the edge before she lets out another deep breath, half moan, half sigh of regret. "I think I need to go. I'm sorry. This is all new to me and I wasn't expecting this tonight. And . . . well, I'm driving. Gotta stay safe. Good night, Derrick."

Before I can say a single thing to stop her, she hangs up. *Damn it, Derrick! You pushed her too far, too fast.* I literally just did a show about listening, not going beyond your partner's limits, and I just blasted past Kat's, lost in my own desire.

My brain is yelling at me, disappointed that she hung up, but my cock is still at full attention, begging for release. I let the image of Kat take over my mind, not even knowing what she actually looks like, but imagining her pink pussy dripping as she rubs a vibrator across her clit.

I reach into my briefs, taking my cock out and grabbing it in one fist, then stroke up and down my shaft, giving me instant relief as I groan. To hell with it. As hot as I am, this will be fast, so the odds of anyone catching me are slim. And if they do, well, they're in for a sight because I can't stop.

I imagine Kat holding the vibe to herself as she slips two fingers into her pussy, thrusting them in and out in time to my own strokes, her eyes hooded with lust and watching my every breath.

In my head, I talk to her, telling her to fuck herself with her fingers. To show me how much she wishes it were my cock filling her tight pussy, how she wants to squeeze and milk me until I fill her up with so much cum that it spills out of her, too much for her little cunt to hold.

The combination of memories of her voice and my own mind filling the gaps and imagining dirty talking to Kat sends me over the edge. I explode, my come coating my hand as I jerk, getting every last shudder from the orgasm as I picture Kat screaming my name as she's lost in her own pleasure.

I glance around my office again, seeing the box of tissues on the corner of my desk. I grab a handful, glad there's something to help clean up this particular spill . . . and damn glad nobody's around to see the mess I've made.

CHAPTER 4

KAT

"*Y*o, Kat!"

"You already spent that new bonus check?"

I huff, wishing I got a bonus check, but I play along anyway. I give a wave to Harry and Larry, two of my co-workers. "You'll see when the pizzas come in at lunch!" I joke back.

Harry rubs his Monday shirt, a stretched and faded *Pizza The Hut* custom job he got off the Internet. "Just remember, no sausage!"

"That's not what I've heard," I tease, and Harry snorts. He claims to be a ladies-man love machine, but I have more than a sneaking suspicion that's all talk and some serious next-level self-aggrandizing. He's a good guy, though, and he doesn't take anything too seriously.

"Yeah, well, hope you've got another doozy cooked up,"

Larry says. "My latest game's gonna have me taking your shine soon enough."

I laugh and head to my cubicle. I've finally gotten it exactly the way I want, with triple screens that allow me to code, visualize, and debug all at the same time.

I immediately pull up my next project, an ambitious attempt at totally integrating calendars, social media, and office apps that could turn the whole damn system on its head.

I need to focus because the coding on this is going to be tricky. Integrating all these systems is easy. Doing it without turning someone's smartphone into a brick that works at the speed of a turtle? That's tricky.

As I work, I know I should be focusing on code. Every line has to be correct and every phrase has to be perfect. I can't have any mistakes or any clogs. But instead, my mind keeps wandering back to my phone conversation with Derrick.

The conversation had been nice until it got a little too heated. I mean, he had me half moaning even before he said what he did. I can't believe I just bailed like that.

Sure, I know I was a total coward, but I truly wasn't expecting it and I didn't know what to say. Especially since all of my blood was rushing to my neglected pussy, making me squirm around in my seat and tempting me to pull over right then to take matters into my own hands once again. I was this close to telling him exactly what I needed.

Face it, Kat, you wanted to, my mind tells me. *In fact, you wanted him to be there, his silky voice telling you what to do, talking you through every action as his eyes watched you with rapt attention.*

Shaking my head, I try to get back to work, putting in hour after hour of work and making little progress. Coding is a lot like speaking a foreign language. For some people, those folks who get paid big bucks, they can translate on the fly, able to listen in one language and talk in another almost instantaneously.

Others, like me, might be just as fluent in both languages but can't operate in both at the same time. So for me, coding means I have to put my brain in 'code mode' to really get in the groove.

Just as my left-hand monitor flashes me a signal that it's noon and time for lunch, my phone rings. It's my sister Jessie, who's learned to never, ever call me during my work hours unless someone important is dying.

Jessie's always been like a second mom to me. Eight years older, we never really had that period when she was a teen where she thought taking care of her little sister was a pain in the ass. Instead, she looked out for me, making sure I got my schoolwork done and never letting me veer too far off the path into crazy.

She's not some stick in the mud though. Actually, the first time I ever got drunk was with Jessie, and we both have had plenty of good laughs along the way. With hair two shades darker than mine and another three inches on me, she's beautiful and a stellar wife and mom, all the while holding down a full-time job as a risk management specialist for an insurance company.

She's truly Super Woman and everything I want to be when I grow up, whenever that'll be. With my new promotion, I'm at least *halfway* there, the professional success coming more readily than the personal. "What's up in the land of vehicle recall calculations?" I ask her. "Got anything that'll blow up in my face?"

"Very funny," Jess says with a laugh. "Actually, I called to say congrats on work and your promotion. Good job, Sis. I knew you could do it. Acing it at work, and on the home front too? How's Kevin?"

I wonder for a split second if she can read my mind, the professional-personal discrepancy coming out of her mouth just a beat after it crossed my mind. I can tell she doesn't care but feels like she should ask.

"What about Kevin?" I ask, trying to not sound snippy. Hell, maybe I should listen to her more because she was spot-on with him and has been right before about boyfriends too. "There *is* no more Kevin."

"What do you mean?" she asks, and I tell her about our breakup, leaving out the issues with our sex life and focusing on his cheating and my not putting up with it.

When I finish, Jess gives me a little cheer. "Good for you, girl. You're beautiful *and* smart, and there's no reason you should have to put up with any man who can't see that."

"Well, I don't want to be a downer, but not everyone finds a fairytale Prince Charming who loves you like Liam does you. Gonna be honest here. He's the only thing giving me hope that such a man exists in the real world, because all the ones I run into are cheaters, liars, and users looking for a booty call and nothing else."

Jess knows my experience with men so she gives me a pass. "He's out there," she tells me reassuringly. "You'll find him soon. Probably when you least expect it."

Unbidden, my mind jumps to Derrick and how that was so unexpected. But I don't even know him. Not really, just his radio persona, although he did seem genuine and real when he was listening to my drama about breaking up with Kevin.

Of course, he seems to have a bad boy side too. Good guys don't start talking about how they want to watch me toy my pussy on a second conversation unless they've got at least a decent naughty streak running through them.

There's a part of me that wants to get my own bad girl vibe going . . . kind of. I mean, I want to, but my wild child streak is sadly narrow, but maybe I could learn a few things from Derrick.

"Yeah, well," I finally say, not wanting to go down that particular rabbit hole at the moment, pun intended, "either way, I'm single now."

"Sexy and single," Jess replies. "Whatcha gonna do with all that ass inside them jeans?"

"I'm wearing a skirt today, actually," I retort. "But I do need to get some lunch."

"I gotcha," Jess says, letting it drop. "Listen, don't let any of those cretins you work with have a heart attack because your beautiful ass goes walking by, okay? And if anyone tries to grab anything, you break their wrist with one hand and slap a sexual harassment lawsuit on them with the other."

"I will," I promise her, smiling. "See you later, Jess."

"Will do. Call me tonight. We can catch up on Mom," Jess says. "Love ya, Kat."

"Love you too. Bye."

---

*G*etting home tonight, I can't help it. I find myself listening to Derrick's radio show.

"Good evening, listeners, your Love Whisperer Derrick King here, and tonight, our topic is something that seems mysterious to most men. Some men say it doesn't even exist."

"The stupid bastards," Susannah says with an exaggeratedly venomous tone of disdain, making me chuckle.

"I wouldn't say stupid, just . . . uneducated and in need of some enlightenment," Derrick purrs, making the muscles on the insides of my thighs tremble. Oh, what this man could educate me on.

"So tonight, our topic is The Female Orgasm. We're going to start off with an email. This is from . . . H. H writes that she and her girlfriend have sex often, but she is frustrated that her girlfriend can only climax from a dildo or a strap-on. H feels like that's off limits. What can she do?"

I lift an eyebrow. Derrick's chosen a doozy to start the night. "Sounds like someone needs some dick," I murmur to myself before my body whispers back that yes, it does need some dick.

"H," Derrick says, his voice sure and slightly stern, making my mouth go dry, "first, penetration has nothing to do with sexual orientation. What your girlfriend needs is what she needs. There's nothing wrong with her body saying that's what it likes best. It has nothing to do with how she feels about you as a person or her attraction to you. I'm just going to be straight with you. What your email tells me is that you might need to deal with your own insecurities. Talk to your girlfriend. I'm sure you two will be just fine."

I'm hanging on to his every word, and I idly wonder if perhaps my confession to him last week inspired this topic.

"Susannah's got us another caller, Z. Z, go ahead."

"Yeah, D, listen . . . I'm trying my best with my lady, but it seems like no matter what I do, she just doesn't get there. Like, we have sex and stuff, and she says she enjoys it, but she rarely has an orgasm. It's messing with my head and I really want to please her."

In his velvety voice, Derrick tells the caller to take his time and he's gotta build up to the main event with foreplay, not just dive in and pound her and think that'll do it.

45

"It starts in the mind, talking to her and telling her how sexy she is, what you want to do to her," he purrs. I can't take it anymore. I can feel my nipples tightening in my t-shirt and I cup my left breast, imagining Derrick telling me this face-to-face.

"Cup her face in your hands and kiss her gently at first, then devour her. Move down her neck, maybe tease a little nibble to see if she's into that, and lick along her collarbone. Make it down to her breasts which by now should be full and heavy," he says, and I echo him, massaging both of my breasts. It feels so good I have to sit down on my couch, leaning back and my legs spreading slowly.

"Tease her nipples, palm them and circle your hands, cradle her breasts and lick the nipples until they tighten up, then suck them deeply. If she liked the neck nibbles, maybe light bites or easy pinches here too. Your mileage may vary with that because everyone is different. Make your way down her body, layering kisses with licks and sucks along the way."

"Fuck," I moan, my eyes rolling up as my pussy quivers in anticipation. I let my left hand slide down, cupping myself through my shorts, the heat making me gasp at the first touch. The whole world swims away and all I can hear is Derrick's sexy growling.

"Compliment her pussy and let your hot breath warm her as you let the anticipation build. Then lick her with a flat tongue from slit to clit several times before focusing on her clit for circles. I've heard writing the alphabet with your tongue can be good, and when you find a letter that makes her moan, do that one over and over, but if that's too much, just trace patterns and rhythms. Flat tongue, pointed tongue, fast, slow to see what she responds to best. The answer's easy really, just pay attention to her. Take your time. Take as much time as you need to help her get into it. You'll be able to tell. She's not gonna be shy about it and you'll know. She'll open up like a flower."

I can't take this anymore. I slide a hand inside my panties, rubbing at my lips and wishing it were Derrick. I bet he's got strong fingers that could leave me dripping with desire and a tongue that could write poetry on my clit.

"Eventually," Derrick continues, "slip a finger inside slowly and pull it out, teasing her opening and stretching her. Hell, who knows, maybe two or three fingers or more. Like I said, just pay attention. Curl them toward her front wall to slide across her G-spot if you can find hers."

I follow his words, slipping two fingers inside my soaking pussy and pumping them slowly before finding my G-spot. Derrick's got me so turned on that finding the spot is easy, and each intense stroke leaves my toes curling on the carpet.

"All the while, you finger bang her and you lick and suck her clit like a starving man. It might take a few minutes, it might take a lot longer, but you do what she likes and stick with it until she comes. It'll be the best reward ever, trust me. After that, well, you see what it takes. She'll be open to you. Just listen to her body and be creative. No wham-bam, thank you, ma'am. Most women are more complex than that, all right?"

Susannah interrupts, and I can hear it in her voice that she's turned on too. "Wow, Derrick. That was rather . . . descriptive. Fellas, from a female perspective, let me tell you . . . hell yes to all of that. Hell. Yes."

They laugh, sending the show over to a song, and Mazzy Star's *Fade Into You* comes grooving out of my radio. I keep my fingers going, pumping them in and out and finding all the ways that my body likes it, grinding the heel of my hand against my clit before easing up and brushing it with my thumb.

The whole time, I can only imagine that Derrick's there doing it. I don't even know what he looks like, but holy fuck, I don't know if it matters when a man knows what he knows. My pussy clenches around my two fingers as I strum my clit with my thumb, and I cry out, pushing myself over the edge and coating my hand in my sweet slickness. The orgasm's intense, and I bite my lip hard, moaning his name. "Derrick."

Fuck me. God, I want him to fuck me so badly. When I come back to reality again, I realize the commercial break's over, and I take my hand out of my soaked panties, panting shakily.

Holy Shit, Derrick's cohort is right. Hell yes to all of that. Listening to his voice describe how he gets a woman to come, giving but always in control . . . it's worshipful mastery and I want it.

I want it so badly.

I definitely should not have hung up last night. Kicking myself for my cowardice and the missed opportunity, I click off the radio as Derrick moves on to another caller who apparently wants to know why his girlfriend can't come from anal.

I can't take another answer from Derrick. Not if I want to get any sleep.

CHAPTER 5

DERRICK

The restaurant is full, but not too busy as I scan the tables. It doesn't take long to find my target. After all, there aren't too many six-foot-five, two hundred and eighty-five pound men who have a build like my best friend.

"Jacob!" I call, seeing my friend turn. He's so massive, I didn't even see that he was talking to someone, a petite blonde girl who's looking up at him with one purpose in her eyes. Jacob gives me a nod and turns back, scribbling a signature along with something else on the piece of paper the girl's holding before sending her on her way.

"Good to see you, Derrick!" Jacob says as we embrace like we did back when we were roommates in college. It was a pure chance pairing, two jocks, one on the football team and one moving away from the sport, but it clicked.

"You too. How's the shoulder treating you?" I ask.

"Not as bad as the sportswriters made it out to be. Mostly

it was just one hell of a bruise. I've been resting it for two weeks now since we've got a bye week. I'm good heading into the rest of the season. Then, of course, contract talks."

Contract talks. Big money. Jacob's coming off two All-Pro years, and if he's going to stay with his current team, they're going to have to pony up some top-flight money this offseason to do it. Everyone's saying the team would be smart to try and sign him to an extension before crunch time.

"Big contract so you can pay for all of your groupies," I joke. "What is it, thirty-two girls for thirty-two cities now?"

"Don't hate the player, hate the game," Jacob jokes. "Green ain't your color, bro. You ain't a Notre Dame fan. Besides, I know that when I find the right girl, I'll settle down. Until then, fuck it. What about you?"

"Not my thing," I admit, sitting down at the table across from him. The waitress comes over, taking our orders, and then I continue. "I'm not gonna hate on you, but that's just not what I'm looking for right now."

"You never were," Jacob admits. "No matter how many times I tried to bring you to the dark side."

"What can I say? I saw the real thing with my parents, and I've never been able to settle for less. Besides, it's not like I don't get out there at all."

"We all heard that. Lookin' for that perfect freak in the

sheets, lady in the streets, I guess. Anyway, I won't bust your balls. How's work?"

"Fine. Been busy, more folks calling in and we can't even get to them all in a three-hour show. But the show seems to be helping people and the ratings are through the roof."

Jacob laughs, sipping his sparkling water. "Yeah, I'm not surprised. I heard last night's show. You probably caused every woman listening to come right then and there. Shit, I'm good, never get complaints for damn sure, but hell, even I was taking notes. Never hurts to up your game a little bit."

We laugh, and I remember what Jacob told me last time we got together. Apparently, more and more of his team-mates are listening in to my show as well. It seems odd that celebs and people I know would be listening to the show, but I do majorly appreciate the support. Somehow, when I'm on the mic, it feels more anonymous. The 'Love Whisperer' is just more of an amped-up facet of my personality, not exactly the real everyday version of me.

"You ever miss ball?" he asks me after we finish our food. "I mean, you helped me train during the offseasons. I know you still had the skills back in college."

I shake my head, leaning back. I remember those days, sweating it out in the winter weight room, the summers running wind sprints with Jacob up and down the steps of the stadium. Even though I'm ninety pounds lighter than him, there were too many times I was a step behind or busting my ass just to keep pace. I had the love of the game, but not that one in ten thousand talent like him. "No, not really. I miss the teamwork, the brotherhood. But it wasn't meant for me. I'm happy where I landed. You?"

He nods, rolling his shoulder unconsciously, and I wonder how much of what he told me about his injury being just a bruise was bullshit. If it is an injury, his season's going to be a lot harder than he's letting on. "Definitely happy. It's a crazy amount of work and I already feel like an old man on some days, but it's all I ever dreamed of."

"I'm glad," I reply honestly. "You think you'll make All-Pro again?"

"Pretty sure," Jacob says with a smile. "You coming to the game tomorrow? Season kick-off?"

I nod, grinning. "It's a hell of a drive, but no way I'm missing it. Already pre-recorded my show for tomorrow. It'll be an all-write-in show so that I can watch my boy get his ass whooped."

Jacob laughs. "Fuck you, man. You know I'm going to be having a party in the backfield."

"I hope you party all fucking night long. I'll be partying right with you if you do."

One of the benefits of being a radio celebrity is that my face isn't as well-known as my name. So as I sit in prime seats, fifty yard line, two rows up, right behind the players, I'm pretty anonymous. If I yelled,

Jacob could probably hear me, but I won't distract him like that because he's at work.

The game is close coming out of halftime, and the tension strums through the stadium. I can see Jacob stretching his shoulder subtly as he leans low to keep his hamstrings warm and loose. He'll be going out with the defense to start the second half and there's a bounce in his step that reminds me how much I loved playing ball.

It started when I was only four years old, throwing a miniball around with my dad, watching games, or at least highlights, since what four year old can sit through a three-hour football game when there were cartoons around, but I loved pretending I was one of the guys on the big TV in our living room.

When I was six, Dad started me with peewee flag ball, the ball damn-near the size of my head. In some ways, I was lucky. Spending four years playing flag allowed me to learn and understand the movements of the game without taking hits. Not that it started that way. For my first year, it seemed every snap the play turned into everyone being directionless ants, running around the field and some-times generally toward someone who had the ball.

Once I got into sixth grade, he let me play a year of Pop Warner ball before junior high started, and the games got more serious. I learned to appreciate the smell of sweaty plastic and to listen for the sound of my parents in the stands, cheering for me. They never, ever missed a game.

It was during the last game of my junior year that I jacked up my knee. I was playing fullback and linebacker for my team—we were that sort of small school. A chop block on my blind side, two pops, and I was down on the grass with a lot of my dreams strained but not yet shattered.

The surgery wasn't much, a quick repair to my meniscus,

some therapy, and I would've been good to go for my senior year. But while it healed, I reported on the playoffs for the little in-school TV program, and I was gone, hook, line, and sinker.

Sure, I played my senior year. I'd put too much into the team and too much time with my boys to just let it go like that. But I didn't eat, sleep, and breathe football like I did before. Dad was disappointed at first, but I'd shown him how serious I was, even interning the summer after I graduated with our local news station as a gopher guy, running for coffees and making copies just so I could be in the excitement of the whole process.

Sitting in my seat, enjoying the late summer breeze and sunshine, watching Jacob and his team fight for victory, pushing their bodies to the limits . . . there's a part of me that wants to be out there. But knowing that they'll be traveling in a few days just to do it all again doesn't make me miss playing.

Maybe I miss reporting sports, but not the actual playing. It was fun to be able to get to know and to watch the athletes, and hell, it was a lot of fun to be paid to watch. Then again, I had a lot of late nights trying to cram a story in to meet a deadline. The job I've got now is a pretty sweet gig, and I can always watch the game without playing or reporting on them. I can be casual and have fun with it now.

The second half kickoff soars through the air, and I sit forward, cheering as Jacob snugs his chinstrap tight. He jogs out onto the field, ready to defend his house.

In this instance, better him than me.

CHAPTER 6

KAT

I pick up my phone for what feels like the hundredth time, my thumb hovering over Derrick's name in my contacts. Since last night's show, all I can do is think about how much I want all the things he described, want to experience them with his silky voice making me putty in his arms.

But even as I'm about to call, I know deep down that although it felt like he was speaking directly to me, that's just his shtick. It's his *job* to answer the relationship and sex questions, use his sexy voice to get all the female listeners hot and bothered, and maybe add a little shock factor to keep folks tuning in day after day, week after week.

I was able to hold out for hours simply because of the announcement at the top of his show that he wasn't taking calls. It's a recorded show, so he may not even be around.

But as the evening's worn on, I can't help but think that maybe he'd *want* to take a call from me. Even as I admit it's a stupid move, sure to end in disappointment, I just have to find out. I'm curious if he used our conversation as inspiration for his show, if he was talking to me, maybe even just a little bit subconsciously.

It rings a few times and I'm on the edge of losing my nerve and hanging up when he picks up the line, his smooth voice instantly putting me at ease. "Kitty Kat. I was hoping I'd hear from you again."

I notice that he knew who I was before I even said anything. That must mean he programmed my number into his phone, right?

I take a second to calm myself so I can sound casual and cool, even as my brain keeps jumping to conclusions that he must have really wanted to hear from me. I clear my throat before answering. "Hey, Derrick. I wanted to apologize for freaking out on you the other night. I wasn't expecting that and I handled it like a jumpy virgin instead of the smooth, mature seductress I am."

I hope he hears the sarcasm in my voice because I'm so far from smooth and mature, it's actually laughable. Despite having a sex drive that I think is pretty respectable, I'm no queen of the bedroom either, even if I have desires to the contrary. Hell, the last time I gave Kevin a blowjob was months ago, and he nearly put my eye out when I jumped back because he came without warning me first.

I'm good with swallowing, but it's considered polite to

give a girl a little head tap as a warning so she can catch a breath first. Instead, I ended up sputtering, my left eye burning from a blast right in the eyeball and a rug burn on my ass that stuck around for a week. So yeah, I'm totally smooth and mature. Not. I mentally sigh at my lack of game.

Derrick's chuckle is deep and rumbly, and it makes me feel like not only does he see through my sarcasm, but he's ready to have fun with it. "I feel like you're making fun of yourself here, but I'd be willing to bet that's more true than you realize. You just need a partner you feel safe with to explore how smooth . . . or rough . . . you'd like to be."

Two sentences. Just two sentences, and hearing the implied challenge, my body's instant response is a resounding 'yes, yes, yes.' I decide to be coy, adding a flirty tone to my voice. "Perhaps you're right. Maybe I do just need the right guy. Do you happen to know anyone?"

There's flirty and then there's jumping in the deep end, and I'm definitely jackknifing about two inches above the surface as I wait with bated breath to see if this really is as deep as he's letting on or if I'm going to crack my head open and have to back out in total shame.

I hear him swallow, the gulp audible through the line in the prolonged moment before he growls in my ear, turning my knees to jelly and my nipples to diamonds. "Where are you right now, Kitty Kat?"

I stammer, shocked that I'm brave enough, horny enough, or stupid enough to be doing this. But fuck, I need him like I need air right now, even if all I really know is his voice. "At home. I–I worked from home today."

I have a flash of a thought that maybe he's going to demand to come over, and that seems a little too real even as my pussy flutters in excitement at the idea. Still, my nerves are screaming, waiting for his response. "Good, good," he says, making me lick my lips. "I just got home too. Go to your bedroom for me."

With a tinge of regret mixed with excitement, I realize that I've never told him my address. He *can't* come over unless I tell him. This is something different, something I've never done before, but as much as I want him and need him, I'm completely on board even if I am feeling in over my head a bit already.

I try to reassure myself. I'm a grown ass woman and this isn't all that unusual, if Elise can be believed. I can do this. Worst-case scenario, I make a fool of myself, hang up, and never talk to him again. Best-case, this could be just what I need. There's no worries about a relationship here. Intimate, but totally secure because it's casual. There's no concerns of whether he's going to cheat on me because there's no commitment to be more than just this. Faceless, no strings, just his velvet voice softening all the anger and disappointment from the last few weeks, getting me off and making my pussy throb in the best of ways. Resolving myself to go through with this, I feel a thrill of excitement rush through me.

Walking quickly down the hall to my room, I sink into the fluffiness of my soft white comforter, perching on the edge of the bed. "I'm here. What about you? Where are you?"

There's a sound in the background of someone walking, then a settling sound before Derrick replies. "I'm in my bedroom. I'm lying back on my bed, propped up on the pillows. What are you wearing?"

I look down at my dowdy work-from-home outfit of a tank top and Winnie the Pooh pajama pants that's decidedly unsexy, and I decide to lie. I don't want to kill the mood. "I'm wearing a sexy pajama set with little boy shorts and a crop top. The boy shorts keep riding up, showing more and more of my ass."

Derrick laughs a bit, and I can hear the grin in his voice. "Kitty Kat, I don't want you to create some fake story about what you think is sexy. Right here in this moment, all I'm thinking about is you and what's real. What do you *really* have on?"

I smirk, knowing I'm busted but somehow, the fact that he wants the truth puts me at ease and sends another little flutter through my belly. "Loose pajama pants and a black tank top. But . . ." I bite my lip, letting the tease build for a split second before continuing, "I don't have a bra on. The girls are free, perky under my favorite black tank."

"Mmm, that's more like it. A natural woman is always better than some fantasy," Derrick says, making my breath catch. Does he understand that he's a fantasy himself right now? If he does, he's not letting on. "How big are your tits? Small little handfuls, medium ripe melons, or large mouthfuls I can bury my face in and feast upon until my lips ache? Be real."

I look down, knowing that I'm curvy in all the right places, but I want to do this right, whatever the hell that means. "They're definitely more than a handful. I wouldn't say they're huge, but I'd love for you take in a mouthful and suck and lick them."

I can hear the tension in Derrick's voice at my little secret, and he hums for a moment. I can imagine him adjusting himself, picturing me in his head. "Take your shirt off and tease your nipples so they're stiff and achy for me."

As I do what he asks, a small sigh escapes my mouth, and I know he heard it. "That's it, Kitty Kat. Imagine your hands are mine, running through your cleavage and pinching those needy nipples." I whimper, rolling my left nipple between my fingers and watching the dark pink nub turn almost red. "Soothe the shock of pain away. You're not gonna hurt yourself. Just enough to let the sensations mix."

I keep rubbing, arching my back into my own hands as I flip it on him. I love feeling the warm touch of fingers on my skin, but I want more. "Your turn. Take your shirt off."

He chuckles, adjusting himself by the sound of it. "Already done, Kitty Kat. I took my shirt off when I told you to."

Feeling bold, I follow up, my knees parting on their own as I undo the bow tie at the waistband of my pants. "All right, move your hands down your chest and belly to your waist. What kind of pants do you have on?"

There's the sound of a belt buckle being released, and in my mind's eye, I can see it, black leather and shiny as it dangles from the belt loops. "Black denim Levi's."

Black denim? Holy shit, he knows just what to say. "Slip them down and off."

There's a rustle on his end of the line, then his voice comes back strong. "Kat, I'd ask if I should take my underwear off too, but it seems that the same way you were letting your tits free, I'm commando over here too."

The thought of him lying naked in his bed is doing crazy things to my head and especially to my body. I smile to myself, knowing I want to push him the way he pushed me with his questions about my breasts. My pussy flutters in my panties as I mewl like a kitten, hungry for him.

"Is your cock just enough to fill me up, maybe more than I can handle, or a monster I'm gonna choke on?"

I know I hit my mark when he groans, and I can almost imagine him reaching down, holding himself and trying not to stroke. "I bet you could handle me. I'd stuff you so full of cock you'd feel places touched that you never even knew existed . . . but something tells me you could handle everything I could dish out. Am I right?"

"I'm no extra-small, teeny tiny thing," I admit. "Is that a problem?"

Derrick purrs, and when he speaks up, his voice is raspy, thick with desire. "No, I like a woman with some curves, hips I can dig in and hold on to. I'm stroking it for you now, up and down my shaft, spreading out my precum and thinking about your pink pussy, imagining how wet you are right now. Slide those pajama pants off for me, Kat."

I do as he says, settling back against the pillows as he tells me to spread my legs wide and trace my fingers across my heated pussy.

"God, Derrick, I'm already so wet. My panties are . . . fuck, you've got me soaked. Your words, your voice . . ." I trail off as the pleasure gets too intense for my brain to multi-task, my focus gathering on the slide of my fingers across the drenched cotton.

"Slide your panties to the side. Let me help you make that beautiful pussy feel good. That's the way your whole body should feel, Kitty Kat. So good and ready . . . ready for more. Rub from top to bottom. Let your fingers spread your honey all over your lips and up to your clit. Tell me how that feels, Kat."

When my fingers find the bundle of nerves, I can't hold back the moan, which rises until I can barely breathe. "Mmm, right there. Derrick, what are you doing to me? How does it feel so good with your voice washing over me, telling me what to do? Are you touching yourself still? I want you to feel this with me. Stroke your cock slow and tight."

Derrick's moan is deep, rumbling and making my fingers speed up a little. "Fuck, yes, I'm touching myself. Your breathy sighs and moans are so damn sexy. I'm imagining it's your hand stroking me. I don't know how much longer I can hold out when I know your needy pussy wants me to fill it up. Is that what you want? You want me to fill you up?"

Incoherent, I moan, but he hears my meaning loud and clear, and I can hear his breath quicken. "Slip your fingers inside for me. Imagine it's my cock thrusting into you, every thick inch stretching you and taking you right to the edge."

I do as instructed, my palm grinding on my clit with every press of my fingers inside. "Fuck, Derrick . . . yes, fuck me just like that."

My hips are bucking, helping my hand, and I ride so close to the edge. I know the sounds I'm making are guttural, but they're out of my control and Derrick is echoing them back in my ear, taking his pleasure as I find mine.

"Faster, Derrick. Fuck your hand like you'd fuck my pussy, pounding into me hard, bottoming out deep inside me." I pant, barely holding on. "I'm about to come, and I want you to come with me."

I can hear the smile in his voice and the tension in his breathing. "Kitty Kat, I've been holding back as much as I can, letting you get there. As soon as I hear the sounds of you coming, I'm a fuckin' goner. I'm gonna nut all over my hand an instant after you come on yours. Together."

In my mind, I picture him pumping his hard cock, his eyes squeezed tight and tension through every muscle as he holds onto the edge for me. I can see him shiny with precum dripping down his shaft and wanting me, and his stomach muscles are tensed, ridged under his skin with the repressed power inside him.

I hear him growl at me. "Kat . . ." And it feels like a warning that he's reached his threshold. When I imagine his come coating his hand as it rushes out of his cock, it's all I can take. The orgasm crashes over me in waves, the cries loud even to my own ears.

Faintly in the background of my climax, I hear Derrick's grunts and know he's coming with me. I tease it out as long as I can, eventually forced into taking a big breath to settle my body from the intense release.

"Wow," I half whisper in total wonder. That was the most intense orgasm of my life, to the point I can almost feel a cramp developing somewhere in my hips because I was bucking so hard and squeezing so tightly. "That was . . . you're fucking amazing."

Derrick laughs, and I'd feel bad except . . . he's out of breath just like me, and I know he's just as shaken as I am. "Mmm, yes it was. You sound surprised. Have you ever had phone sex before?"

I shake my head before remembering that he can't see me, and I giggle lightly. "No. Never. But definitely checking that off my bucket list now."

"How about you don't mark it off, and maybe we can do that again?" Derrick asks.

"I might take you up on that," I reply, biting my lip. Late-night sessions with the Love Whisperer? Lucky me.

There's a moment of comfortable silence before my brain kicks in and I remember why I called in the first place.

Well, I remember the excuse I used to justify calling. "Hey, can I ask you something?"

"Shoot," Derrick replies easily, and I feel another notch of comfort with him. He's not trying to cut the call short now that he's gotten a little action. No wham-bam, thank you, ma'am here. Vaguely, I wonder if he's the rare type that actually likes to cuddle. He might be an actual freaking unicorn . . . sexy, sweet, and dare I say it, nice. "What's up?"

"This is silly, but . . . I listened to the shows this week. The female orgasm topic seemed rather on point."

Derrick laughs softly, and another little tremble goes through my belly. I could listen to that throaty rumble all fucking day. "Yeah, you got me. You mentioned that in our conversation, and it made me think about how many women are not getting what they need. If I can help one guy be a better, more considerate lover and one woman have the orgasm she deserves, I'm calling that a successful show. Thank you for the inspiration. And I'm sure that somewhere out there in the city, there's at least one woman thanking you too."

Me, an inspiration and a muse? He knows how to make me feel even sexier. "See, and here I was thinking you just wanted to get all of us ladies turned on. I bet power companies all over had to fire up an extra reactor for the electrical surge from all the vibrators turned on as soon as you finished that bit. Hell, it sounded like your cohort had to run to the bathroom to rub one out before continuing the next call."

He laughs in that way that tells me something else. Whoever his coworker may be, he's not interested in her. He's not calling her up late at night and causing her to come her brains out. "Susannah? Definitely not. Most of the time, she barely puts up with me, but she does a great job of keeping the show on track. She's the real backbone. I'm just the pretty voice. As for the rest of the listeners, I don't know. I just hope to help, I guess."

I smile, realizing he does seem like a truly nice guy, with a sexy voice and an unabashed sex drive. I feel a shot of warmth through my cynical heart, a drop of hope for mankind taking hold before I remember that Kevin was like that once too. Actually, several of my boyfriends were.

Too many men in my life start off charming and kind, on their best behavior to get you to relax around them. They made me laugh, they were warm and built trust until I let my guard down, and they found purchase in my heart. I didn't mind, of course. I thought everything was cool until they used that foothold to rip my life to shreds, leaving me spinning, wondering what happened.

My mood darkens, even as my body still hums with satisfaction. Trying not to let the change show in my voice, I try to lighten the vibe. "Ah, noble Sir Sex-a-Lot, riding in on his steed to save the citizens from a woeful lack of romance."

He laughs at my comment, and I can tell at least this one time, I fooled him. "Well, maybe not quite that dramatic, but something like that. Hey, you asked a question. You mind if I ask you one?"

"Sounds fair. I keep the bodies in the attic."

Derrick laughs, sending another thrill through me. "I'll be sure to remember that. But . . . would you mind if I texted you during the days too? I mean, I've got your number, after all."

I smile, lying back on my pillows. "I'd like that."

CHAPTER 7

DERRICK

I'm floating, trying not to get too far ahead of myself. But the mere fact that Kat called me back and was equally engaged in our phone proclivities makes me smile.

Part of me can't believe it really. It's been so long since I found a woman interesting, and I was beginning to wonder if my work had made me jaded. I've certainly had several serious relationships, in college and after, but for one reason or another, they weren't the one.

All except one were good women. I tend to be a decent judge of character, but things never really clicked. I couldn't picture myself with them decades from now, happily hanging out and still chasing each other around the room to get frisky.

I don't even really know Kat yet, but something tells me that she's worth getting to know to see if she has potential to be the one.

There's a shy sweetness to her, even as she stands strong against a shitty boyfriend and says dirty things to me. It's an intoxicating combination. It's been a few days since our late-night session, but even with our conflicting schedules that have her working days and me working well into the evening, we've found time to text. A lot.

There's an anonymity to sitting behind a small screen, a disconnect that somehow lets you feel like you really know someone while simultaneously making it easier to spill your guts because there's no eye contact. There's always that built-in safety net of stopping the texting.

But we've never stopped, and sitting at my desk now, I've got my phone out, tapping away.

Hey KK, I text, my shorthand for Kitty Kat. *What are you doing?*

It's only moments before the reply pops up, making me feel good. *Work stuff. Nothing fun like you.*

I smirk, dipping into the naughtiness that's become a regular for us. *Oh, you want to do me?*

Funny . . . I meant your work is fun. She sends back after a moment. *Mine's dry & I'm rushing to my latest deadline.*

Dry, huh? Well . . . I bet I can change that. *I could distract u. Maybe make things a little less . . . dry. Maybe even slick and wet.*

So tempting . . . so very tempting, but I need to get this done. What's tonight's topic? Should I tune in?

Message received. You want to talk but can't afford to get

naughty. That's okay, there's later. *Always. I like knowing you're listening. I don't remember what the show is about tonight. We do the whole week's schedule at once & I forget. Languages of love? BDSM kink? One of those.*

LOL . . . those are very different topics.

Almost as if she were here, I shrug as I type out my reply. *Not really. Both about open communication & respecting ur partner's wishes.*

If you say so, Kat sends back. *I guess I'll have to listen.*

I glance up and see the clock, hissing at the time. *Gotta go. Pre-show meeting has probably started without me.*

I see her kissy face emoji as I slip my phone into my pocket, smiling as I enter the conference room. Susannah raises an eyebrow as I sit down. She's always one to dress nice, especially nicer than my usual jeans and t-shirt, but she's dressed even better than usual in a creamy silk blouse with understated gold jewelry at her neck and ears. Wonder what's up with that, who she's trying to impress? This is radio, after all. We could do this in our pjs and listeners would be none the wiser since they can't see us. "Nice of you to join us, Mr. Love Whisperer. Something more pressing than tonight's show?"

She's scolding me like she's my boss. There's even a thinly veiled trace of anger in her voice, and I wonder why she's so upset and behaving like a snarky child. Shit, I'm less than five minutes late for the meeting, and beyond a refresher on the topic, I don't need any more prep. I'm ready to roll like I always am. I attempt to defuse, showing

I'm on board. "Nope. Here and ready. What's tonight . . . love language or BDSM?"

She clucks, obviously surprised I knew what was on the agenda and disappointed that she doesn't get to ream me out. Looking down at her checklist, she makes a mark with her pen. "Technically, it's called *Languages of Love* tonight. Remember, we're doing an on-air interview with the psychologist who wrote the book. She's hot shit on the Amazon market and there's talk she might end up on New York Time's Bestselling list by year end. So we're basically a big commercial block for the book without sounding like an infomercial. Here's the monologue for the top of the show explaining it all, along with a background on her so you don't stumble into any issues. I picked emails to highlight each of the points she wants to cover so we need to hit those as a priority over phone calls."

I take her typed notes, skimming the psycho-babble descriptions contained in each section. Boring as fuck, honestly. It takes me fewer than ten seconds to realize that whatever this lady has to say, it could be summed up in two paragraphs written in really little words. Ah well, guess my job's the same. "Emails are the priority. Got it. Hey, Susannah?"

She looks at me, her eyes still flinty. "Yes?"

"Thanks for this. There's more here than usual. I can see you pulled a lot together for tonight's show, and I'll try to do all of your hard work justice," I say, but not just to assuage her hurt feelings. She's a good co-worker and does do a great job of keeping me on track, especially with a fancy topic like this. I'm more of a 'love her well and treat her right' kinda guy, but obviously, some folks need a bit more guidance, and I'm glad Susannah is here to make sure I don't do something stupid like contradict the author.

She really is the glue that keeps the show successful, even if her work is more behind-the-scenes. There've been several times she's had to feed me good advice for a caller when the questions got a little beyond dark and into *whoa* territory. I have a pretty broad 'book knowledge' at least on most things, including some of the darker sides of sexual relationships, but I've always been sort of the 'good guy with an edge.' Nobody's ever accused me of being the bad boy.

That's one of the ways Susannah balances me. She's dabbled in a lot of things I haven't, or at least she comes off as familiar with them in a way I'm not, and she's always focused on making the show the best it can be while I focus on helping the most folks. Without her driving us and scheduling topics, I'd have run out of shit to say months ago.

I see her soften, and I know despite the hard-edged bitch persona she likes to project, she's got a real side to her too. "Sure thing, Derrick. We've got this. C'mon, Love Whisperer."

There's a teasing note back in her voice, and I know whatever made her mad about my being late is settled, or at least pushed to the back burner. Susannah is an utmost professional, and she's ready to rock this show with me like always. "Good. Now, what's the schedule for the other upcoming shows?"

"Like you ever remember?" Susannah says, and I smirk. She's right.

"Amuse me," I retort. "Imagine that I actually am a professional at this, and forget to remind me that I'm an idiot tomorrow and the rest of the week."

"Don't I always?"

CHAPTER 8

KAT

"*A*nd that, ladies, is why you should always tell your man where exactly you want him to bury his tongue. That's what I call 'quality time.' Am I right?"

I was just getting my dinner ready and missed the opening segment of Derrick's show, but now, as he gives advice to a woman who wrote in about her partner's oral skills, I have to set my fork down before I drop it on the floor. The deep intensity in his voice sends a shiver through my body even as he talks to the whole city. It feels like he's talking just to me.

Setting the bowl of pasta down, I hold my breath, not sure if I'm listening to *Languages of Love* so I can get to know Derrick's heart a bit better, or *BDSM* to get to know his sexual leanings better. I've never been into hardcore BDSM, but the way Derrick speaks . . . maybe a little spanking wouldn't be too bad at all.

Of course, there's always a degree of fakeness for the airwaves. Derrick's careful. He's not going to divulge too much personal information, but he always manages to weave enough of himself into the advice he gives that you can't help but get to know him. So I keep listening, mixing in the little tidbits he tosses the listeners with the information he's shared only with me . . . and liking what I'm finding more and more.

"Okay, here's an email from Lexus," Derrick says. "Now, I'd like everyone's opinion on this one. It says, 'Dear Love Whisperer, I've been with my boyfriend for three years now, and I've got a problem. You see, I only really feel like he loves me or gives me attention when he buys me things. For the first two and half years of our relationship, he bought me diamonds, pearls, even a new car for my birthday. Recently, though, he lost his job and he's tried to make up for it with what he calls 'little things' like cooking me breakfast in bed or drawing me pictures, but it doesn't feel the same. What should I do?' "

"I have no idea what *she* should do," Susannah says, "but if I were Lexus's boyfriend, I'd be thinking it's time to trade her in and see if there's a better ride that doesn't cost so much."

"Hold on," Derrick says, barely holding back his laughter.

I snort, thinking Susannah's right. But the special guest tonight butts in. "I disagree," she says in a haughty voice. "It's obvious that Lexus has felt a lack of dialogue with her partner as their situation has changed, and she must take the initiative to make sure both of their needs are being met on a level they agree on—"

Derrick interrupts, his tell-it-like-it-is self not wanting to wait his turn. "Let me put it to Miss Lexus straight. I get that some people feel loved with gifts, surprises that let you know your partner was thinking of you and wanted to give you something to make your day a little brighter. But hell, honey, it sounds like you're venturing into gold digger territory here. It seems like you don't want a boyfriend. That's a relationship of partners, of equal give and take across all areas of your life. That's what it sounds like your boyfriend's tried to do. I'm curious how many late bills he's accumulated to buy you those diamonds and pearls. Unless he happens to play second base for the Red Sox, I would think quite a few."

"Now, hold on—" the guest says, but Derrick is on a roll and wants to finish.

"Sorry, just one second. Lexus, what you want is a sugar daddy, someone who will just take care of you and spoil you. And just so it's clear, there's nothing wrong with that. Just recognize what you really want and set out for that. Find someone who gets his joy from buying you things."

It's surprisingly good advice for a listener who sounded rather unlikeable from the whiny tone of her email. Maybe they were a little harsh, but with an email like that, it's hard not to get a little snappy.

With that, the show goes into a song break, the recognizable beats of Iggy Azalea's "Fancy" blasting out of my speakers. Feeling light and happy, I dance around my apartment a little bit, the song infectious and making me laugh at how decidedly *not* fancy I am.

I'm mid-twerk, dropping it down at the start of the second verse when my phone dings on the table, signaling a text message. I'm surprised to see it's from Derrick.

U listening? Just had a doozy.

Always listening, I text back, smiling. *U kno I'm ur #1 fan. Btw, can you buy me a Benz, Daddy?*

Stop it. I'm on air. Can't laugh yet. Suz is still pissed at me.

Then y r u texting me?

Song break. Was thinking of you.

I smile, the simple idea of him thinking of me while he's supposed to be focused and attentive at work somehow making me feel good.

He's all I think about too, playing and replaying the phone conversations and texts over in my mind. I bite my lip, knowing I shouldn't do what I'm considering. This is going to take things to a whole new level, but it's not too serious.

U want something to really think about?

There's a bit of a delay, and in the back of my mind, I hear the song change over from "Fancy" to "Yeah!" by Usher. Nice transition.

Song says it all.

Fuck it, if a man is willing to send me messages through the radio, I'm doing this. I slip into the kitchen where there's better light and pull my V-neck tee down, revealing the deep line of my cleavage and the pretty floral bra I selected this morning because I was feeling extra sassy.

I snap a pic from above, being smart while doing something totally crazy and making sure nothing else is in the shot. No face, no room, nothing identifiable. Ensuring it's flattering and anonymous, I click *Send*, along with the note, *think about these.*

I've never done this before, but he makes me feel so wanted even though I've never met him face-to-face. And something about the whole thing with Kevin makes me feel like taking this risk, like it's a common cultural phenomenon I've somehow never participated in and am maybe missing out on. This is a fuck you to Kevin, an invitation to Derrick, and a shout from my spirit that I am the head bitch in charge of my destiny. Seems like a lot to ask from one spontaneous shot of my breasts, but I have to admit, they do look great from this angle.

The response comes back so quickly that I know he's watching his phone like a hawk. *Holy shit, KK. So fucking hot. Look at that, they're begging me to taste them and mark them as my own. Bad girl, gonna make it hard for me to focus on the next segment because all my blood is rushing to my cock.*

I smile, glad that it worked. This is a big step for me. And a big step in whatever this is I'm doing with Derrick. Phone calls and texts are not the same as real-life pics, and I'm well aware how quickly a simple pic can send things into a tailspin.

But I'm not cheating like Kevin was, and I'm not trying to get more out of Derrick. I'm just having a bit of fun. I'm single, he's single, and it's all good.

Right?

Give me a call later. Maybe you can see . . . more.

CHAPTER 9

*M*y pulse is racing in my veins as I set my phone aside, my throat suddenly dry at the thought of what Kat just said.

Holy fuck, did she just invite me to see her? I'm going to be hard-pressed . . . wait, I'm already hard. But more to point, after the beautiful set of breasts that I just saw, I'm going to have to do my best to be semi-gentlemanly. Gotta at least see what color her eyes are before I dive into those puppies for a suckle.

I look up and Susannah is giving me the evil eye, obviously annoyed that I'm texting during the show. It's not against the rules. We don't have too many rules that we actually have to follow, but it is something I rarely do since my focus is supposed to be work. And during the songs, Susannah and I usually chat about the last caller or sometimes the next segment.

Tonight especially, I should be schmoozing with the guest

author, not pushing that off to Susannah to handle alone. Still, this fucking pic . . . I smile at Susannah sheepishly, hoping the silent recognition will be enough apology to move on as I hit *Send* on one last text to Kat, promising to get her back later.

Susannah's not buying it, it seems. "Who's so important that you're texting them mid-show, Derrick? We've got a lot of information to cover tonight and I need you here with me. You could've at least said bye to our guest, especially after cutting her off."

Something in her tone of voice makes me think the first question was what she really wanted to ask and the last bit about the show or guest was an afterthought.

I shake my head, trying to clear my thoughts. "Just a friend," I lie through my teeth. "She's listening in and we're chatting about the show."

Susannah snorts, shaking her head and making her brown hair bounce. "Lovely. Perhaps you'd like to discuss the show with me too, considering we're still in the middle of it?"

Damn, what's up with her tonight? First the pre-show meeting and then busting my balls about texting Kat. For the first time ever, I'm ready to get off the air and out of here.

"My bad," I reply, trying to keep it light. "Let's keep it rolling for the rest of the show."

"Of course. Just keep your head in the game. We've still got two hours of show left, several more emails to read, and callers too. You can't just drift off whenever you want." She's back to chastising me, not responding to my semi-apology.

She's riled up now, almost ranting. "We have to stay focused so the show doesn't bomb tonight. The bigwigs will be listening to see how we handle a guest that's a paying advertiser, and so far, it wasn't stellar. She's gone, but we still have to do a few plugs for her. Pull it together, Derrick, so that we represent the book effectively." She rolls her eyes. "In case you didn't know, or care, advertisers are how we actually make money for the station."

"Fine," I snip as I move back into position for the next bit. Maybe I was off my game tonight, but I don't need her bitching me out. "Let's get this done."

———

*I*t's a lot later than normal when I get home, but it's all I can do to get inside before I'm texting Kat again to see if she's still up. I've been thinking about this all fucking night, and after the night I've had, I need this. I want to see more of her, but I don't want to scare her off either.

As soon as she responds, I hit dial, calling her. Her voice is like a shot straight to my dick, breathy and low and purring like the sex kitten I know she has buried deep inside her. "Hello."

"Kitty Kat, you don't know what you've done," I growl, yanking my shoes off and sitting on the couch.

I'm so heated that I realize I made her worry when I hear the apprehension in her voice. "What? Did I get you in trouble at work?"

I know the pic had to be a big leap for her, and I appreciate that she did that with me, *for* me. Quickly, I reassure her. "No, Kitty Kat, I'm not the one in trouble. *You* are. Because all I have been able to think about are those tits."

Kat's voice is lighter now, playful as she realizes everything's more than okay, and she's been waiting for this too. "Oh, really? Seems I did get promised a little something in return that I haven't gotten yet. I have to tell you, Derrick. You're my first. I have never done something like this, so go easy on me."

I growl, something about her teasing about my being her first making my cock grow to full hardness in the blink of an eye. "Hang on, then. I have something for you."

I lean back on the couch, pulling my shirt up and my pants down to grab my throbbing cock in my hand and snap a pic. I check to make sure it's showing just how thick and hard I am for her and hit *Send*. "There you go, Kitty Kat. That's what you do to me."

I hear her breathe in as the pic comes through on her end and she sees what she does to me. "Damn, Derrick," she gasps, her voice quavering, "Is all of that for me?"

We're starting to slip into this with ease, the buildup from multiple get-to-know-you texts and flirty jokes making the initial awkwardness a thing of the past. "All yours, Kitty Kat. I need you to do something for me tonight."

"Anything," she replies immediately. The lack of hesitation makes me shake, knowing that she's with me, whatever I say next. "I want to see you. I want to see you come for me. Can you FaceTime or Skype me, Kat? Let me see you."

There's a long, silent pause on her end, and I wonder if I scared her. "Derrick, I don't know. I've never done anything like that and I'm not done up. What if . . ."

She trails off, and I'm eager to put any concerns she may have at ease. "What if what? It's just you and me like it was before, turning each other on."

Kat sighs in my ear, her voice quiet and insecure. "What if you don't like what you see?"

I laugh. This woman is crazy in a good way. "Kat, I already know I'll like what I see because it's you. I've pictured you a million times already, in all different shapes and sizes, and they're all sexy as fuck because they're you. I just want to see you for real. Are you saying that if I'm old and fat and hairy, you'll never want to talk to me again?"

I wait a split second before I continue, "By the way, I'm none of those things, in case I just scared you." When she chuckles a little, I know she's relaxing and I can tell she's thinking about it.

I hear her take a big breath, and I'm already prepping for the no I know is coming when my phone beeps.

Oh, yeah, this what I know we both need. She's changed our phone call to a video call. My pulse pounds in anticipation, palms sweaty. I know it's intense, but I'm so ready to show her just how intense I can be and still keep her within her comfort limits.

A huge smile breaks across my face as I accept the call, and a split second later, I see her.

Kat's eyes are huge, the brown orbs wide with nerves, but she's stunning. Her honey blonde hair falls in messy waves down around her bare face like she just pulled it out of a bun, and she's wearing the same V-neck t-shirt from the picture earlier.

There's no way to describe her except to say that she's an angelic dream. So fucking beautiful.

She waves shyly, and I realize neither of us has said anything yet. Finally, she finds the nerve, even if her voice is small, worried that perhaps I wouldn't accept her. "Hi, Derrick."

I smile widely, both at having a face to match to the pure eroticism of her voice and also in surprise that this gorgeous woman would ever doubt that she is the epitome of sexiness. "Hello, Kitty Kat. I don't want to sound trite, but . . . you are stunning."

I watch as she bites her lip, obviously not really believing me but pleased with the compliment nonetheless. Her eyes race across my face, taking in my wavy dark hair, blue eyes, and my trimmed beard. I have a moment of uncertainty, hoping she likes what she sees too.

"You too," she finally manages. "Well, not stunning. I mean . . . you're handsome. Hot."

The last bit comes out quieter, like she meant to only

think it but it slipped out anyway. It makes me smile, but it's softer, and I lean forward, setting my phone on my coffee table. "You okay? We good?"

Kat nods her head, her smoldering eyes on me through the screen driving me insane. It's like her body knows what she wants, and most of her mind knows it too . . . but she's got something that's pulling her back. "Yes. I'm okay."

I grin, planting my elbows on my knees and watching my screen like a hawk. I smile before continuing. "Take your shirt off, just like before. Show me those tits I've been dreaming about all evening."

There's a jostle on her end as she props the phone up and steps back, letting me see more of her curves. I swallow as I take her in.

She's about average size but has a thickness to her in all the right places. I don't even realize that I haven't said anything yet so she speaks up instead. "Derrick?"

I hear the uncertainty in her voice and finally drag my eyes back up her body slowly to meet hers, "Damn, Kitty Kat. You are so fucking sexy."

I see her chest rise and fall as she takes in a breath, for courage, I think. I consider encouraging her more, but I back off slightly, wanting this to be her choice. I want her to want to do it for me as much as I want her to do it, so I stay quiet, my eyes rapt on her, telling her everything that I want.

After what seems like an eternity but is probably really

just a few seconds, she pulls the t-shirt hem up and over her head, revealing that she doesn't have on a bra anymore.

Her breasts are full and ripe with deep pink areolas surrounding her hard nipples. I pull my eyes away from the mesmerizing force of her nipples to scan down her body, across her nipped-in waist, soft tummy, and curvy hips to her pussy covered in black bikini panties.

They're functional and basic, not designed for seduction but oh, so sexy anyway. The high straps curve up and over the swell of her hips, making the whole visual even sexier. My cock throbs with hunger to feel what she'd feel like against me, under me.

Somewhere deep inside, I like that she's not *done up*, as she called it, not some fake version of herself that only highlights the good stuff. This is really her, just hanging out at home in comfy clothes and no makeup, and she's letting me into her life for a moment, vulnerable and real. For that, I can only say one thing. "You're absolutely stunning. I know I said that already, but this is better than I've imagined."

She blushes but smiles. "Thank you."

"Can you touch yourself for me?" I ask, transfixed by the image on my screen. "I need to see you . . ."

I watch as she traces her hands up her hips, across her waist, and up to cup her breasts, lifting them up and together. As she does, the uncertainty and shyness vanish in increments as she gets more aroused and comfortable with what we're doing.

My eyes lock on the image before me, my mouth watering as I fantasize about licking her luscious mounds. I hear her make a noise, a soft moan of desire mixed with an admonition. My eyes shoot up to meet hers, and she's smiling at me.

"Nuh-uh, Derrick," she says, *tsk*ing me. "This isn't one-sided. I want to see you too. Take your shirt off."

I don't even think. I reach back to grab my shirt and rip it over my head and off. The cotton stretches but holds enough that I don't embarrass myself by just Hulking out of the shirt. I slide my fingers across my chest and down my stomach, letting her see where I'm put together.

"You have tattoos," Kat mentions, looking at the ink work I had done in college. "I wasn't expecting that, for some reason."

I nod, looking at my left arm and ribs, the intertwining designs still something I like. "Do you like them?"

Kat's eyes gleam and I recognize that she's turned on. Not necessarily by my tatts, but my questions. "I guess I've never really thought about them before, one way or another, but right now, I want to trace them with my fingers and tease and tickle you as I draw every line across your arms and chest."

I do what she suggests, tracing the lines I have memorized from seeing them in the mirror every day, closing my eyes and imagining it's her soft touch. I hear her breathing hitch, and I open my eyes to see her drawing circles around her breasts, getting closer with each round to her stiff nipples, her back arching to chase her own fingers.

"Fuck, Kitty Kat. Are you ready? I need more." She nods, giving me permission. "Can you sit down somewhere? Prop the phone up so I can see you spread wide for me."

"Yeah, hang on . . ." There's a bit of shuffling, and the phone swirls wildly around her room, but I'm too busy ripping my pants off to get a good look at her apartment.

In a moment, we're both settled back down on our couches, the phones propped on the tables in front of us, and we're both flushed with anticipation. Kat looks nervous again, excited but definitely a bit anxious. It makes her even more beautiful, the light flush of her skin letting her feel real to me. I lean forward, taking her in. "Kat, you okay?"

Her breasts shudder as she takes a deep breath, causing my cock to throb but also something else to move inside me. This woman, she's one of a kind. "I am now," she finally says. "Just . . . this is so hot. Crazy. And hot."

I grin, letting her see just a hint of the bulge in my shorts. "Rub your tits for me again. Show me exactly what you want me to do. Get back in the moment, here with me."

She does as I say, the tension leaving her body as she responds. "You too. Lean back. I want . . . I want to see."

I smirk, knowing she's with me now even as she stumbles a bit in her demand. I lean back on the couch, easing my underpants down until my dick comes into her view through the screen. Her breath catches, and I wrap my hand around my shaft. "This? Is this what you want to see? My cock hard for you? Because fuck, I'm rock hard for you right now."

I give myself a few strokes, spreading the precum across the head and down my shaft as she watches. I see her pinch her nipple a bit, and the sound she makes forces me to squeeze myself tight to stop from coming right then.

"Fuck, Kat," I gasp, trying to hold on. "More . . . I want to see your pussy."

She bites her lip, pausing for a second before adding a pillow behind her back and adjusting to lift her feet to the table edge out of my view. She's laid back, her pussy close to the screen and her body rising up in perspective from her wide hips to her small waist, to her lush tits, and to her flushed face. She smiles dreamily, her hooded eyes looking down her body at me. "How's this? Can you see?"

"Oh, I can definitely see," I reply, my hand moving slowly up and down my cock again, totally of its own volition. "I can see everything a man could ever want. I can see your pretty pink pussy, so wet for me it's leaving honey on your thighs where you were pressing them together. Touch yourself, Kat. Tell me how wet you are."

Her fingers move down, running up her inner thighs to brush lightly across her lips. "Mmm, I'm soaked, Derrick. I need more. Fuck, I need . . ."

Without my telling her to, she starts to trace her fingers through her lips, slipping up to coat her clit with moisture as she swirls a circle around and then begins the pattern over again. Something about her knowing her own pleasure and confidently taking it without me is so fucking hot. She's in control right now, and I love being the lucky fucker who gets to see her in this moment of strength. I'm still slowly stroking my length, enjoying the sight before me, and I decide to let her stay in charge for now.

"What do you want me to do, Kitty Kat?"

Her eyes pop open to meet mine, and she grins naughtily. "Jack yourself off, Derrick. Fast. I need it now."

Just her words are almost my undoing, so I give my head another squeeze, and with a breath, the moment passes so I can do as she said. I watch her fingers beginning to blur across her clit, and damn, the limits of digital technology because I want to see every detail of her hard nub pulsing as she rubs. "That's it, Kat. Imagine those are my fingers strumming across your slick clit, spreading your juices everywhere I want to touch and taste you. Hold yourself open for me. Show me your sweet little cunt."

I lift my hips, thrusting into my fist in time with her strokes, and I start to groan. Looking up, I realize that as closely as I've been watching her hand, she's been watching me too. Knowing that she's turned on by my body, my hand sliding up and down my shaft does it and I can't hold back. "Kat, fuck, baby. I'm gonna come. Come with me."

She cries out, her head falling back and her eyes rolling as her orgasm overtakes her. Seeing her so gone like that is all I can take, and I come too, the thick ropes slicking the way for the last few strokes.

We catch our breaths, our pants slowing as we come back to awareness. Kat's eyes are wide as she sits forward, robbing me of the beautiful sight of her pulsating pussy but at the same time gifting me with the flushed, smiling face of this angel I just came with.

"Fuck, Derrick. I don't think I've come that hard in . . . well, maybe never. I thought you tore me apart last time, but this time was even more intense."

She's done, already satisfied and settling, but I'm roaring inside. That orgasm was probably the hardest I've ever come too, but it's not enough. I need more. I need her. I know my voice is full of gravel, every touch of my trademark velvet gone as I'm filled with lust.

"Kitty Kat," I rasp, staring into her eyes. "I know I said it earlier, but I need you. Let me come over. Fuck, I need your sweet pussy."

She blinks, then grins. "Here's my address. Hurry."

CHAPTER 10

KAT

I sit back, my still-damp thighs trembling, whether in fear of what the fuck I just did or in anticipation of what the fuck is about to happen, I'm not sure.

Oh, my God, I told him yes. Derrick "The Love Whisperer" King, the sexiest man on radio and the sexiest man I've ever laid eyes on, is on his way to my apartment right now.

What am I doing?

I need to . . . something. When I told him my address, he said it would take him fewer than twenty minutes to get here. He told me not to get dressed, to stay just like I am, but sitting here is killing me.

I know. I'll call Elise. Probably a good idea for someone to know that I have a stranger coming to my house anyway, but she'll tell me if this is crazy or not because it feels crazy. Making sure I've turned off my camera, I dial her number, running my fingers through my hair as it rings.

"Kat," she greets me, not surprised at all that I'm calling her this late at night. "What's shaking, baby?"

"Elise, this is urgent. I need your advice."

Elise's voice immediately sobers, and I can hear her sit up. She's probably been binge-watching TV again. "What's wrong? Need something?"

I run my fingers through my hair again and decide that staying ready for Derrick doesn't mean I can't brush my hair and teeth. I head toward my bathroom, talking all the while. "Okay, so I'll try to make this long story really short because time is of the essence here. You know the radio guy, Derrick King?"

Elise chuckles. She was the one who turned me on to his show to begin with. "Oh yeah, the Love Whisperer. Let's get it oooonnnnnn."

She says it with the full effect of Marvin Gaye singing the ultimate sex song, but I'm not in the mood to laugh. "Yes, *him*. So I called in a couple of weeks ago about Kevin."

"You did what?" she says, shocked. "I know it's hard, Kat, but you have to let him go. Kevin is a total douchewaffle and you deserve so much better. I can fix you up with someone if you want. Maybe we could even double-date?"

I roll my eyes, loving this girl, but sometimes, she needs to be quiet and let me finish. If not, she's going to snowball the whole time Derrick's driving and I won't get any advice. "Elise. Stop talking for a second and lemme finish. This isn't about Kevin. It's about Derrick."

Elise stops mid-word when she realizes what I just said, and when she speaks again, her voice is rapt with attention. "Sorry. Continue."

"So I called, and he told me to dump Kevin and then told me to call him back personally because he was interested in how it turned out."

"I didn't know he did that," Elise says, surprised. "That's surprisingly nice for a radio semi-celebrity."

I find my hairbrush and start running it through my hair, smoothing out the tangles. "He *doesn't* do that. He did that . . . with me."

Elise hums knowingly, already deciding she knows where this is going now. "We-he-hell, now, you just made my night interesting."

Great, I made her night interesting. Meanwhile, my previously semi-behaving waves are now a knot of tangles where I thrashed my head against the couch. Definitely some freshly-fucked hair going on here. I grab my spritzer bottle and lightly spray the back, detangling the mess gently so it doesn't frizz out like an electrified poodle. "So I called him back, and we got to talking, texting, and other stuff."

"Oh, and what 'other stuff' is my oh-so-shy but oh-so-beautiful friend talking about?" She knows what I mean, and I don't know if I can say it out loud, but I need advice, so I try to charge ahead like this is normal, no big deal for me.

"Fine, we've been having phone sex, texting dirty innuendos, and tonight . . . tonight, we had sex on FaceTime."

Elise is clapping, cheering in my ear like I just won an Olympic medal or something. "That's awesome, Kat! Welcome to the 21st century. Everyone does this, you know. How was it?"

I'm blushing. Apparently, I'm behind the times if this is supposedly common. Maybe I'm reading too much into it? At least my damn hair is starting to look decent again.

"Well, it's been great, really great. But tonight was different. It was . . . wow. I don't even know what to say, but that's why I'm calling. I've never, ever come so fucking hard, and at the end . . . it was like epic or something, and now he's coming over! What do I do?"

"Uh, wait a minute," Elise says, stuttering a bit at the end. "You had phone sex and *now* he's coming over? Have you ever met him face-to-face?"

I hear the tone change in her voice, and I know she's worried about something. "No, is that weird? You know I have no idea what I'm doing here. I've barely dated, just one semi-long relationship after another. And I certainly never had phone sex before. Is it not common for him to come over afterward?"

Elise sighs, but like the supportive friend she is, she gives the truth as she sees it. "Uhm, honey, that's definitely not the norm. Usually, it's just an awkward bye after you're both done with business. But if it was *that* good, and you like him, hell, this could be a good thing."

I set my hairbrush down, picking up my toothbrush and stopping just as the drop of green gel is a fraction of an inch about the bristles, listening. "A good thing?"

Elise chuckles, but it's not derisive. "Yes, a good thing. You need this, Kat. It's not serious, you're not jumping into some fairytale here. But some wallbanging sex with a hot man to get over the last douchcanoe is just what you need. Oh, wait. He is hot, right?"

I feel something icky on my thumb and realize my drop of toothpaste has become a veritable splooge of minty freshness, and I quickly put the tube aside, flicking the majority of the junk into the sink. "He is so fucking hot, Elise. I couldn't have programmed a hotter man."

"Now I'm jelly," Elise replies with a chuckle. "Not too jelly, but jelly."

"I was nervous he wouldn't like me after he saw me."

"Honey, I'm not gonna listen to a word of that," Elise growls as I start to brush my teeth quickly. "You're a fucking gorgeous woman, not some twiggy pre-pubescent little girl. And any man worth your time will not just accept your curves, but he will drool for them with appreciation."

I laugh, feeling a little better, and spit into the sink before answering. "So you think this is okay? I'm not being stupid?"

"Yeah, babe. You're good. Just don't get too tangled up,"

Elise advises. "Use this for what it is . . . some hot sex to rebound, a nice casual hookup. Not some Disney shit where he's going to sweep you off your feet."

I know what she's saying, but she doesn't have to worry. "You know I don't believe in that fairytale crap anyway. The last thing I need is some guy playing me for a fool again. I think I've finally learned my lesson."

I hang up with Elise, feeling more confident in the whole thing but nervous because I'm about to have sex for real for the first time in months, and I don't exactly have a good track record with guys satisfying me.

I look at myself in the mirror, hoping I'm not playing myself. I'm hoping Derrick will be different because somehow, this feels different. I may not believe in getting swept off my feet romantically, but something tells me Derrick might be able to knock my socks off.

Well, if I were *wearing* socks.

The knock on the door comes almost too quickly. I barely feel like I've finished rinsing my sink out. Padding in my bare feet to the door, I take a big breath, still deciding whether I'm going to go through with this. Maybe I just don't answer and I'll never have to face the reality of this.

But I know I'll fucking regret that for the rest of my life. I'll never know just how good Derrick can make me feel. There's this nagging feeling inside me that for the first time in my life, I've got a chance to meet a man who will satisfy my every carnal desire, to take my body places that I've never imagined it could go.

Forget the humor and sweet conversations we've had that make my spirit lighter and my heart clench in my chest. Forget the fact that every time I talk with him, I'm left smiling for hours or that even a short text from him can bring a little twitch to my lips. I focus on the need deep in my core and make my decision.

Just sex. That's all we're doing and all I need. If we can be friendly too . . . that's great. I can't expect more as I stand here naked, not getting dressed like he instructed, and I open the door to find Derrick standing there, his breath coming in fast pants and his eyes bright with lust.

He presses a hand to either side of the door frame, not coming in yet, but if I wanted to leave, I'd have to go through him to do so.

"I thought you weren't going to answer for a second. Are you not as sure about this as I am?" He seems like he's on the edge of control, ready to burst into my apartment and take me. It's a heady sight to see him so close to the edge . . . over me.

I shake my head, biting my lip to keep my nerves and insecurities inside. "You don't see any clothes, do you?"

He smiles. "The whole way here, I've been picturing you under me as I pound into you, you straddling me to ride, the taste of your sweet pussy, and you on your knees, sucking me down. God, I want you every way you'll let me. I want to know you inside and out. If you don't want that, tell me right now and I'll go. But if you let me in, neither of us is going to be the same again."

Every word from his mouth is like he's weaving a spell

around me, his voice dripping with sex and turning me on as I picture all the things he describes.

I lower my hands away from their protective stance, showing off my naked body to him and anybody else who happens down the hallway. Fortunately, it's late and the hallway is empty. I'm somehow more upset that someone might see the thick tent Derrick has going on in his pants than I am about someone possibly seeing me nude in my doorway.

His cock is mine, just for me. And that's what does it for me. I want this. I want him. I dip my head once, and it's all the affirmation he needs to rush me, slamming the door behind him as he grabs my ass, lifting me to straddle his waist.

His lips meet mine in a desperate kiss, nothing soft and sweet. This is instant fire spreading through me as our bodies meet for the first time. His touch is electric, his lips devouring mine as he carries me deeper into my apartment, so worked up that we don't even make it to my couch but instead, he presses me against the wall.

Our tongues tangle, fighting to lessen the heat but only serving to intensify the need pulsing through me. He kisses to my neck, sucking and licking at my ear, jolts going through me with every stroke.

"Where?" he growls, my lust-overloaded brain lost for a moment before I realize he's asking where I want him to fuck me.

"On the left, end of the hallway," I groan, tugging on his

hair and looking him in the eye, any uncertainty blasted away by his presence. "Fuck me, Derrick."

"God, yes," he says, striding with me in his arms. His grip never loosens, and I feel secure in his arms as I lick down his neck, nibbling on the thick cord of muscles connecting to his shoulder. He groans, squeezing my ass and grinding my pussy against the hard ridge in his pants. "Fuck, Kat. I don't think I can wait. I need to be inside you. I swear I'll take care of you, but I need to feel you surrounding my cock."

God, I want that too, and I mewl out my agreement as we reach my bedroom. He lays me down on my bed, moving down to taste my neck with licks and sucks and then to my nipples, hard with desire.

He swirls his tongue around before sucking my breast in deep, pulling draws. Shit, that's new and awesome. He moans, the vibrations deep in his chest rumbling against me.

My body writhes in waves, my tits lifting for him to suck at me more, before I shudder and my pussy lifts, begging silently to be filled. It's beyond my control as the surge of desire flows through me. I don't know how much longer I can wait to have him inside me. "Derrick . . . I can't wait any longer. Fuck me."

Too soon, or maybe not soon enough, he lifts away, standing up to grab a condom from his back pocket before stripping naked. He's even sexier standing in front of me, his skin tanned golden and his tattoos rippling over top of his muscles. Suddenly, he freezes, both of us fully able to take the other's body in for the first time.

"My God, Kitty Kat. You're even better in real life. I can't wait to feel you."

I spread my legs, letting him see, using my fingers to open up my labia just for him. "Derrick, fill me, please."

I hear the begging plea in my voice, but I can't even care right now because if he wanted me to, I'd damn sure get on my knees at his feet to beg and not feel a bit of guilt about it. He doesn't seem to need it as he strokes his shaft a few times, opening the condom with his teeth and then rolling it on.

I watch, mesmerized, and slip my fingers down to play through my folds, relishing the way his eyes widen and lock onto my now-wet fingers.

Climbing onto my bed, Derrick grabs my hand. "That's my job now, Kitty Kat. I've got you, but fuck, I need your taste on my tongue when I fuck you." He lifts my coated fingers, inhaling my scent before licking and sucking them into his mouth. I moan, the thought of him tasting me on my own fingers doing strange things to my suddenly dirty mind. "That's it, taste me."

For a good minute, he savors me, his eyes never leaving mine until we're both gasping with need. Reaching down, he takes his cock in his hand, rubbing it along the length of my slit and coating himself, teasing my clit and preparing me for him. "That's it, cover me, baby, mark me with your honey. I could come just rubbing my cock against your little clit, Kat. Does that feel good?"

The circles he's drawing on my pussy with his cockhead are driving me wild, and I chase him, moving my hips to get him where I need him. "Ready, Kat?"

I nod, and he thrusts inside me in one deep stroke, filling me completely. Inside, he pauses to let me adjust as I cry out, the stretch both sharp and so good all at once. I begin to move, rolling my hips as my fingers dig into his forearms, pulling him down. I need more. I need to feel him pressing me into the mattress and dominating me with his strength, his masculine essence that nobody's ever been able to bring enough of before.

Derrick takes the cue, beginning to press in and pull out slowly but powerfully, bottoming out deep inside me on every stroke. His body presses into mine, my breasts flattening against the hard muscles of his chest, and I wrap my arms and legs around him, drawing him in tighter.

"You're so tight, Kat," Derrick rasps in my ear. "It's like you can barely take me. Please tell me I'm not hurting you."

I'm barely able to string a coherent thought together, so I use my feet to urge his hips closer to mine, rambling, "Not hurting, just so good. Fuck, Derrick . . . I don't think I've ever been this full." My rambles die out into breathy hitches with every thrust of his cock into me.

I see him smile and know I said the right thing. He keeps pressing inside me, and I tighten my grip, letting my fingers roam over the muscles that stretch across his back. He covers my mouth in a kiss, holding my hips still as he stays deep, grinding into me. "You can take me, Kitty Kat.

You're squeezing my cock just right. You're fucking milking me every time you fuck me back."

I tense my inner muscles, lifting my hips to meet his, the rhythm becoming frantic and my movements becoming wild. Derrick pulls back slightly, slipping a hand between us to strum across my clit, and I cry out. "Yes!"

"Keep telling me what you want, Kat," he growls as he strokes my clit. "Do you want me to tease your needy clit, barely brush across it, or do you want it slow and steady? Maybe fast and hard?"

As he says each option, he demonstrates, progressing from a feathering touch to soft circles and finally to a blurring stroke. It doesn't matter. My orgasm is building with every thrust, every caress of my clit, and I squeeze him, loving it.

"Yes! I'm coming," I cry out, and he pinches my clit firmly, the sharp sting mixing with pleasure as he pounds into me. It shatters me, my body flying apart, and I buck wildly beneath him, my hands grabbing for the blanket to keep me grounded. Somehow, I'm floating away, white sparks flashing across the blackness of my closed eyelids.

From far away, I hear Derrick panting, his voice growling and wondrous at the same time. "Goddamn, Kitty Kat. You're damn-near choking my cock. Keep squeezing me like that and I'm gonna fill you up. Your pretty little pussy, so full of my come until you can't even hold it." The idea must trigger something for him, and his whole body tightens as he holds himself deep inside me.

He roars as the orgasm takes him, and he loses the

rhythm, his body jerking as he comes. I lift against him, taking over the rhythm to help him ride out the pleasure as long as possible until he collapses onto me, our gasping breaths mixing as we smile at each other.

He lifts up to kiss me gently but thoroughly before he pulls out slowly, both of us groaning. I feel the immediate loss of fullness and already wish he were inside me again. He steps out to the bathroom to handle the condom and I take a big breath. It's late, and after the two best orgasms of my life, both of which shockingly happened in one night, I can't keep my eyes open.

He walks back into the bedroom, and there's no need to ask, and even if he did, I think my open arms answer the question well enough. Snuggling up, we drift off together, and it's probably less than ten seconds later before I'm fast asleep.

CHAPTER 11

DERRICK

I t feels a little weird to be getting dressed up for a first date with a woman I've already seen naked and had sex with, but that's what I'm doing. Weirder still, we're getting ready for our 'first date' while the sun is still up. With my job making me a consistent night worker and Kat's job leaving her with a lot of flexibility as to when she does her work, it just seemed natural to have our date now.

There's a cool early fall wind ruffling the collar of my leather jacket as I get out of my car and head toward Kat's building. It's not the fanciest apartment building in the city, but it's cozy. It suits her, not flashy but somehow just right when you pay attention and really see its charm.

I walk up the stairs to the third floor, nervous for some reason. It's not like we don't kinda know each other. After all, we've talked and sent messages back and forth for weeks . . . and we've rocked each other's bodies to the point that I'm aching while still wanting more.

But this is different. This isn't a late-night video chat and booty call. This is a *real* date, and there are *real* consequences to this.

In the days since our little impromptu sleepover, we've been almost mentally inseparable. Text messages have led to phone calls. Phone calls have led to flirting and even one more late-night rush over here to tear our clothes off for hot, pulse-pounding, brain-rattling sex that has shaken me to the very core.

So here we are. We're both off work tonight and I'm picking her up for our first real date. Maybe we're going at this whole thing backward, sex first and getting to know each other after, but I'm determined to play on the attraction we've had from the beginning because no one has intrigued me quite like Kat has in a very long time. She deserves—hell, *we* deserve—a proper date with fancy clothes, dinner, and a walk around the park. A date where we're going to talk face to face, where all the nuances and details can't be hidden behind emojis and blurry screens that lag at the most inopportune moments.

Knocking on her door, it feels strange to have her open up and see that she's not half-naked or more, her full breasts heaving with desire and her eyes sparkling with need.

Instead, when the door opens, she looks . . . almost shy. Her beautiful hair is pulled back in a ponytail and her eyes are guarded, like she realizes something is different, special about tonight too. "Hi."

"Hi," I reply, nervous as well. I look her over and realize one of the biggest differences. Every other time I've seen

Kat, she's been barefoot. No idea why that's what I notice first, but I do.

She's wearing sky-high heels, at least six inches tall, her poor toes nearly bent ninety degrees in them. Her jeans hug her thighs and hips, showing off her curves in delicious relief. Her left shoulder peeks out of an off-center sweater that looks soft and inviting, making my palms itch to pet it.

"Would you like to come in?" Kat asks after a moment, and I understand. I've been standing in her doorway like an idiot, ogling her. "Uhm, if there's time."

"No rush," I reply, giving her my most reassuring smile. "Actually, the place I picked out was in the park. You might want to change shoes."

Kat looks down, blushing. "But then I'll be short. I thought these heels were . . .sexy, and I didn't want to look so short next to you."

I blink, surprised, and say the first thing that comes to mind. "I haven't minded your height when your ankles have been wrapped around my head."

Kat blushes more deeply, then laughs. "Good point. Okay, well, fill me in on the plans and I can adjust."

"I thought we could go down to Jordan Park. There's a restaurant that gets great views of the pond over there and has some of the best crab soup in the entire city. Other good stuff too, if you're not up for crab."

"No . . . I love crab," Kat replies, smiling. "Did I tell you that before?"

"No, but you mentioned something about seafood once, so I ran with it."

Kat smiles and goes to change into some more appropriate shoes, wedge-heeled boots that still bring her up a few inches but aren't going to have her walking a tightrope down the sidewalk. We head downstairs, and I do a slight double-take when she reaches into her small purse and pulls out her wallet. "Wow . . . what is that thing?"

She looks at the device, which has carbon fiber sides and a couple of other high-tech looking things on it. "Nerd moment. It looks a little intimidating, but I'm just techy. My wallet is RFID scanner secure, waterproof, and holds my IDs, cards, and work access behind an access code. You can never be too safe these days, especially in my industry." She uses a swipe card to let us out of a side door and slips the contraption back into her purse.

I chuckle. "Wow. Talk nerdy to me some more. I think I like it."

She smiles as we start driving, and I feel like we're off to a good start. There's a slight tension between us, but it's casual, not uncomfortable. This is just a new milestone for us. My mind clicking through our interactions like a slideshow, a thought occurs to me. "Hey, can I ask," I say as we pull up to a stop light, "how'd you meet Kevin? I mean, you describe him as this meathead, but you don't seem the type to be into meatheads."

Kat smirks, looking down at her lap and blushing a little. "I guess it's because of my background. I've always been the girl who was more comfortable with tech than people, but even in my area of expertise, I'm an anomaly. Somehow, I'm both an outsider of the boys' club and intimidating because I'm damn good at my job, so I guess when Kevin approached me, it just seemed easy to go along with it. Until it wasn't. Every guy I've let in has been like that, charming but on some level, just meh."

"Well, I promise you one thing," I reply as we start moving again, "I'm nothing like Kevin."

"I would never think otherwise," Kat says. "My past relationships, even with Kevin, were pleasant at first, but there was never any fiery passion. Not like how we seem to be."

For some reason, that gives me a buzz of pride. "If you don't mind me saying, I know what you mean. This isn't how I usually feel either, especially on a first date." I turn into the parking lot at Jordan Park, and we take in the view in front of us. Set aside by a wealthy businessman who wanted to have a little bit of immortality, the park's built on his old estate grounds, complete with a pond, a small river, miles of walking paths, and lots of other stuff.

As she scans, I look at her profile, long lashes brushing her cheeks as she blinks, the corners of her lips turned up in a bare hint of a smile. I want that smile, full-watt and focused on me. My voice is quiet, soft as a cashmere whisper. "I'm glad you realized you deserve more, Kat."

She blushes and looks over at me. "I've never really had this before. You make me feel so sexy."

Inwardly, I shake my head. I don't know how that's possible, but it makes me want to show Kat just how sexy she really is. I lean across the seat, cupping her cheek in my palm and tracing her cheekbone with my thumb before meeting her lips with my own. She sighs, our lips parting as we kiss, stoking the fire that's always burning just below the surface with her. With a groan, I pull back, trying to lighten the mood before I pull her into my lap right here in the parking lot. "Date. We need to . . ." I swallow, looking up at her from below the flop of hair that's fallen in my face. Continuing, "We need to walk. The nerd herd does exercise, right?" I give her a saucy wink, and she takes the hint.

Kat mimes pushing up a set of glasses on her nose and snorts. "Uhh . . . is that where we get all sweaty? My heart rate is rising already."

We get out of the car, and I have to give my cock a thump to get it to calm down so we can start walking. As we move along the sun-dappled path, I can't help but keep looking over at her. Her bare shoulder is close to me, and all I want to do is kiss it, maybe lick the line of her collarbone. My cock starts to harden in my jeans again, and I have to look away before I start perving on her in public. "Derrick?"

I blink and look at Kat, who's giving me another shy look. "Yeah?" I ask, confused.

"I just wondered why you looked away," she says.

Heat creeps up my neck, and I lean in to whisper in her ear. "This is supposed to be a first date, all polite and maybe a little romantic, right?"

"Right," she whispers back. "Why?"

"Because I've spent the last two minutes thinking that you look hot as fuck in those painted-on jeans and pettable sweater, but I know you'll look even hotter in those fuck-me pumps we left back at your place. Those heels and nothing else . . . maybe pinned back next to your ears as I watch you take all of me." Kat blushes and grins, and I move my hand to her lower back.

"I've been checking out your ass in those jeans too, so I guess we're both guilty."

We move closer to each other, and I can feel her hands sliding inside my jacket when music fills the air. I place the tune quickly, *She Blinded Me With Science*. "What's that?"

Kat reaches into her purse and pulls out her phone, holding up a finger while mouthing a *friend*. I step back, inhaling the cool air and letting it chill my burning blood while she talks. "Uh huh? Oh, no, I'm so sorry. I understand. I'll be right there. No, it's okay, babe. Yeah, I am, but he'll understand. Besides, you're my bestie, right? Okay, see you soon."

She hangs up and turns to me, sighing. "You're not gonna believe this."

"There's an emergency," I say, making little air quotes with my fingers, "and you have to go? Is this a fake friend call to get you out of our date?"

We both laugh, and Kat shakes her head. "No, I swear. But my bestie, Elise . . . she's having a man crisis."

"You seem like you've done that before."

Kat looks surprised and snorts. "No, just been the girl on the other end of the line with Elise a few times. Somehow, this time, I'm the rescuer, not the rescuee. This is a little different, which makes it important. It's time to return the favor."

"A woman with her head on straight, taking care of her friends when they need it. I like it," I reply, resisting the urge to ask the obvious question of whether Kat's talked to Elise about me.

She laughs, and I find myself more enchanted with her even as my desire to take her back to bed doesn't diminish at all. "Elise has a wild and crazy side, but most of the time, she doesn't need saving, just uses me to be polite on occasion if the situation calls for more finesse than bridge-burning. She's fun, the yin to my yang, and would burn the world to ashes, no questions asked, to protect me. That's more than even my sister would do."

"What's with your sister?" I ask, tucking every detail away for later. If Kat's trusting me enough to let me know about her background and her family, it's a start, even if we're not getting our early dinner.

"Oh, that came out wrong. She's awesome, just *too* perfect," Kat admits with a laugh. "Jessie's happily married to a great guy. He's the rare one-in-a-million, but she thinks there are carbon copies of him on every street corner just waiting to be picked up. She forgets sometimes about the reality the rest of us live in. Even my mom. She was married to my dad for years, but he stepped out on her all the time. We just didn't know it for a long time. When she found out, she kicked him out, and Jessie and I supported her through the divorce, even when her friends told her she should've looked the other way and made do. I was still a teenager, but I did what I could. Jessie and Mom are really the powerhouses though. I'm just the little sister still figuring things out. Sometimes, I wish life could be like one of my programs . . . organized, predictable, and when an issue comes up, you troubleshoot and resolve it logically, no facades or ulterior motives. Just data."

She looks up a bit, and I feel like of everything she just said, the last part was probably the most insightful thing about her true self. After a beat, she finishes, "Mom's remarrying in a few months. He seems like a great guy, but we'll see. Odds are not in her favor."

Ouch, that's harsh. Then again, with what she's gone through, I guess Kat's earned a few harshness points, and maybe even some cynicism. "I hope for the best. May the odds forever be in her favor."

"Me too," Kat admits, then shakes her head, smiling. "Come on, nice nerd moment there. Now tell me your story while you walk me back to the car. You know, being a gentleman and all, maybe I can bum a ride to Elise's place while you go grab us some caffeine since it's too early for the wine I'm betting Elise will want?"

"Sure," I reply. I'm quiet for a few while I try and figure out how I'm going to answer Kat's question, then I just decide to jump in. Fuck it, I can't help I've had a pretty ideal childhood. "I know it's a little boring, but my parents did well together. They loved each other fiercely until Mom died a few years back, and Dad has said he'll never remarry because he's already had the great love of his life."

Kat smiles, shaking her head in disbelief. "Really? That's old-school romantic. What's he doing now?"

"He's doing okay now, still works hard and has friends to keep him busy," I answer. "He sold the old house—totally understand that—but stayed in town, moving into a little starter home. I go see him a few times a month, more during football season so we can watch the games together. I wish I could go more because he's getting older, but it's a ways out to see him, and he's staying busy and happy."

Kat looks down, looking sad. "I'm sorry to hear about your mom. If anything, she seems to have raised a good son."

I swallow, thinking that Mom would be happy to hear a girl like Kat say that. "It's okay. It was a sudden aneurysm. She didn't suffer, and she left behind a lot of friends, a lot of good memories. I don't think there are too many bad feelings in the world about her."

Kat hums. "That's really sweet, a testament to how she lived. You said your dad is 'getting older'. How old is he?"

"They had me when they were almost forty—tried for years and years. She thought she was going through menopause, but . . . surprise. It was me. They were thrilled, and I always knew how much they loved me. I was a lucky kid, their little plot twist in life."

"Damn . . . your parents were like one in ten million," Kat says. "Does that mean you're the same?"

"I'd like that happily ever after sort of thing," I admit. "Wouldn't you?"

"I've never thought that was meant for people like me," Kat finally says. "It's like catching lightning in a bottle. For most of us, that just doesn't happen."

We get back to the car and I don't really know what to say. I mean, if we're not in this for trying to find something more than a short-lived flash of fun, then what the hell is this all for?

___

*K*at and Elise take forever to handle the man crisis, but they seemed appreciative when I returned with Chinese takeout and wine instead of the requested coffees. I sat by quietly, not sure if my input would be welcome but mostly because Elise didn't need advice, just some support as she bitched about finding out that her slimy boss, who's married, is sleeping with one of the other reporters. Kat had given me a look like, *See? Always happens*. It felt like another nail in the coffin of her perception of reality. Elise hadn't even paused in her rant, going on about nepotism in the workplace and that maybe she should report him to HR, even if the reporter had been doggedly pursuing the boss in a flawed attempt to get better stories. It was draining and lasted until later than I'd thought. The moon is high in the sky and the stars are twinkling as I pull up in front of

Kat's place. I'm thinking the day, and date, are pretty well done.

Kat seems to think so too and looks exhausted as I walk her to her door. "Thanks," she says, smiling softly. "Maybe next time, we can have an actual first date."

"Oh, I don't know," I joke. "I mean, I know all about what's happening in Hollyweird now from flipping through Elise's coffee table magazines. That's not too bad, right? Did you hear about the pregnant Kardashian?"

Kat chuckles. "Which one? I guess I could say that I've had worse dates, but I'm not sure if that's particularly flattering to say." She smirks, and I smile back, happy to find some humor after this decidedly unusual first date.

There's a moment where we just look at each other, and I lean in, breathing in the scent of her floral perfume. "So . . . think I might be able to come inside?"

Kat bites her lip, looking up into my eyes where I see desire building inside her. "That sounds like a loaded question. We're switching gears here, from whatever we were . . . to actually dating. And I don't fuck on the first date, and that's what you said this was. Even if it wasn't epic."

"True, I did say that, but sometimes, first dates end with a little more than a kiss at the door."

Kat blushes, mocking outrage. "What kind of woman do you think I am?"

I pull her into my arms, pressing her voluptuous curves against me and lowering my voice to growl in her ear.

"Apparently, a lot more proper than I thought. I like it, but I also appreciate the naughty side of you that likes it when I talk dirty in your ear and loves to moan my name when I make you come."

Kat's hands wrap around my neck, pulling me down closer. "Well, as long as you can respect me in the morning, you can have a good kiss."

"That," I say as I bring my lips closer for a searing kiss, "is a given."

Our lips touch, and moments later, I'm pressing her up against the door and staking my claim on her mouth. She kisses me back just as hard, clutching at my ass until she feels my cock pressing against her belly. We don't stop until our moans become too loud for the public hallway, and I pull away, leaving her gasping for breath.

"Well, Miss Snow, that was a very fine and proper kiss," I say in a mocking formal accent. "It was such a delight to spend the afternoon and evening with you. I hope you'll do me the honor of escorting me again. Soon."

Kat catches her breath, smirking as she leans in close again. "I'd be delighted, Mr. King. Don't get any ideas though. I'm a lady, and even if you've got a world class cock, I don't *fuck* on the second date either."

She breathily draws out the word *fuck*, intentionally emphasizing it to drive me out of my mind. I pull her close again, groaning as I admit . . . she wins this time. There's a demand, an order in my steely voice. "Say it again, Kitty Kat."

Her eyes are wide, innocent as she looks up at me, her lip quivering and her nipples hard against my chest. "What? *Fuck.* Is that what you want me to say? How about . . . no matter how much I want you to fill me up with that thick *cock* of yours, *fuck* me hard, and maybe even bend me over the arm of my sofa to smack my *ass* . . . I don't do that on the second date."

She's killing me as she accentuates the dirty words, knowing that I love it when she lets loose on those triggers, already so much easier than our first conversation when I had to force her to say 'cock' on the radio.

I grin at her, playing even as desire courses through my veins. "Yeah, *that.* You're playing with fire here. You know . . . you never said anything about my licking your pussy until you soak my face. Maybe that can be an acceptable second date activity?" She giggles a bit and hope soars in my chest. "Maybe I can call you when I get home?"

I kiss her neck, hopeful that somehow, she'll relent, our phone calls being somehow separate from our first date, that she wants me so much she'll give in to a phone call at least. But she's loving this game, and as she runs her fingernails down my neck, she chuckles under her breath. "Oh, no, that definitely wouldn't be proper after a first date. I guess I'll just have to take care of things myself tonight. When did you say our next date will be?"

My brain zeroes in on the image of her pleasuring herself like I've seen so many times already, and my cock jerks in my pants. "Tomorrow night. It'll have to be late because

I've got a meeting with a sponsor as well as the show . . . but fuck, I need it to be tomorrow."

She's driving me wild, this almost dual nature of Kat as she reaches down, cupping my cock. "I can do tomorrow. I'll be listening in after work. Call me around ten or so?"

I nod, reaching up and rubbing a thumb across her stiff nipple. "Ten. Be ready."

Kat smiles mysteriously and gives my cock a final caress through my jeans. "Have a good night, Derrick. I know I will." She says it with a raised eyebrow, obviously teasing me further about just what she'll be doing tonight.

She steps back, closing her door and leaving me stunned. It's not until the brass knocker presses against my chin that I realize I never said goodnight.

I lean close, whispering loudly through the door, trusting that she's just on the other side. "Goodnight, Kitty Kat."

CHAPTER 12

KAT

"*K*at? Earth to Kat?"

The fog of my daydreams lifts as I realize my sister is calling me, and by the look on her face, she's been saying my name for a while. We're taking a long lunch for a family errand. I'm going to work late tonight to make up for it.

"Sorry, what?"

Jessie smirks at me, tilting her voice salaciously. "And what, pray tell, are you fantasizing about, dear little sister?"

Blushing, embarrassed at being caught red-handed, I try to divert the attention away from me in any way I can. "Not fantasizing, you horny bitch. Get your mind out of the gutter. I'm just daydreaming, thinking about work and a new project I'm developing."

She nods wisely before rolling her eyes hard enough to let

me hear the thunks as they hit the backs of her eye sockets. "A project you're developing? Is that what the kids are calling it these days? Take a hint from an old lady. If he's a project model, move on. Guys that need work aren't worth the time. Find a grown up." She freezes, a look of horror shooting across her face. "Oh, God, you're not talking about Kevin, are you? Please say you're not trying to *fix* him. Girl, tell me I'm wrong."

I flinch back, wondering if Elise and Jessie have been sharing a brain or something. "God, no, definitely not Kevin. He's long gone and I've moved on . . . way on."

She smiles triumphantly, and I realize I walked right into her trap. Dammit, that's what I get for being the little sister. "So moved on to . . . whom? What's his name?"

I give in. Besides, I kind of want to tell her anyway. "His name is Derrick, and he's a radio personality. That's actually how we met, but it's not serious. We've just . . . chatted a bunch, and we had our first official date yesterday. So it's all super-new."

I'm relieved when she gloms on to the date part and doesn't question my stutter as I described our late-night phone proclivities as 'chatting,' or to Derrick's job. I mean, how do I explain to my sister that her nerdy, seemingly straight-laced little sister is dating a sex advice expert?

"First date?" Jessie asks, leaning far enough forward that she's invading my personal bubble. "Oh, my gosh, so how was it? Are you going to see him again? When?"

She's almost jumping up and down in her chair as she lobs questions at me faster than I can answer them. It's joyful to watch, and I laugh at her excitement, forgetting my nervousness a little. "It was great, yes, and tonight."

She squeals, making a sound I haven't heard since . . . well, since about the time she got that fan form-letter from Justin Timberlake back when she was in high school. "Tonight! Oh, my gawd!"

As she's still buzzing, our mom steps out of the dressing room behind Jessie. I'm breathless as I take her in, stunning in a soft ivory floor-length gown covered with lace and beading. Jessie sees my face and whirls around, her jaw dropping in shock too. "Well, girls?" Mom asks. "What's the verdict?"

"Mom, you look gorgeous," I tell her truthfully, stepping forward and taking her hands. "Truly. Bob is going to forget his vows when he sees you walking toward him." I mime a fish mouth opening and closing. "The whole church is going to see him rendered speechless."

She laughs lightly, smoothing invisible wrinkles in the dress. "Really? You think it's all right?"

Jessie and I look at each other and then back at her, shaking our heads before Jess speaks up. "No, Mom. It's not *all right*. It's amazing."

We walk around her, taking in all the little details of the dress while Jessie, who's always been the fashionista of our little duo, gives a rundown. "It hugs your hips just right, not so tight you can't sit down, but tight enough to show your curves."

I have to chime in something, so I blurt the first thing that comes out of my mouth. "And the girls look va-voom! Thanks for the good genetics there, Mom."

Probably not the smoothest line that's ever been said, but Mom laughs, posing and visibly more confident in her dress. "Thanks, girls. I don't know what I'd do without you two here for this."

Her eyes fill with tears as she pulls us in for a tight three-way hug. After a moment, she giggles, letting go. "Okay, enough of that. You two are going to get makeup on my dress, and I can't have that."

We step back, standing behind her as she looks in the mirror at herself, but she seems to be talking to us.

"I never thought I'd do this again. Your father . . . well, he really did a number on me. You know I don't like to talk bad about him because he's your father, and we did have a lot of good years together. But there at the end, it wasn't pretty. I hope I protected you from most of that."

We nod, knowing that she'd done her best, but Jessie and I spent many evenings curled up in the same bed as they'd fought, our mother's screams and our father's booming yells the soundtrack more than once. We hugged each other to sleep on too many occasions to be completely fooled by her comfortable lie.

She never told us, but we knew he'd been cheating, had heard her accusations, his denials, and his eventual admissions, but always with some justifying reason why it was Mom's fault that he'd had to resort to that. Even when she would take him back, we didn't understand why, but in some ways, it was nice . . . at least we had peace and quiet again, and a comfortable normality to things. But it tore us apart.

It's why when she'd finally had enough and divorced him, we supported her and cut him out of our lives. Dad didn't understand at first, thinking we didn't know about his affairs and that Mom had poisoned us against him. The letters and even calls from his lawyer as they dealt with the divorce lasted for months, until Jessie had been the mature one to tell him that we knew, we didn't approve, and to never contact us again.

I just avoided the whole confrontation and didn't return his calls until eventually, he stopped calling altogether, much to my relief.

If I learned anything from my father, it's that whatever happiness you get . . . it's just an island in the sea of misery. It can be a big island the size of Antarctica for some . . . for others, it's like a Styrofoam cup floating in the Pacific. And sometimes, you don't know when you're getting too close to the shoreline, and the wave will just crash suddenly and pull you back out with the tide. "Mom, you deserve this. For as long you can have it with Bob, enjoy every moment."

I mean it to sound loving and supportive. It's not her fault or mine that we tend to be Styrofoam cups, but she hears the bitterness. She turns around and comes over to hug me. "Kat, I know you don't understand this . . . but I would happily take one blissful day with Bob over a life-time alone. It's not a risk to love him and let him love me. It's a gift, one that I am blessed to have for as many days as we get. Sure, maybe one day, it'll explode and I'll cry in devastation. But even then, the days of joy will be worth the pain. Even as bad as it got with your father, we had a lovely life for a long time and he gave me the two best gifts of my life, you girls. So yeah, I'll take this happiness for as long as I can have it, without bitterness or cynicism."

I'm taken aback, my mom's words hitting rather close to home. I *am* bitter and cynical. And she's right, because Bob really is a good guy who wants to make her happy.

He didn't have to ask her to marry him, I know. After his first wife died of cancer, he could have just been a rather well-to-do older bachelor. Mom would have been happy just dating him exclusively, I know it. She never asked for his support and didn't need it after she made her way successfully after the divorce. Neither of them needed the other. They just wanted to be together, forever. So when he dropped to a knee on Valentine's Day and asked her to marry him . . . it was totally legit and love-filled. Even since then, he's been great while they plan their second weddings as if they were kids doing it for the first time. There's no reason I should doubt him.

Unfortunately, it's not just my dad's influence. I've had a run-in or two myself.

The good memories with them definitely don't outweigh the bad endings. Kevin was, if anything, one of the longer 'islands' in my history. Some of us just aren't destined for happily ever afters. Or even happy for nows.

Jessie pipes up, ever the optimist. "Maybe this new guy, Derrick, will be the one . . . tonight!"

I turn to Jess, ready to go claws and hissing on her, but Mom smiles. "Tonight? Do you have a date? Is that what Jessie's caterwauling about?"

I try to smile back, but the thought of having a bad ending with Derrick is already pressing on my heart. The fact is, despite whatever guards I've put up about Derrick, I like him already. A lot. We've barely begun whatever this is, but I already know it's gonna hurt like a son of a bitch when it ends.

It's not just the sex, or the fact that he pushes me just enough that I feel like I'm stepping outside my comfort zone without feeling like I just got chucked out of an airplane with no parachute. It's in the way he looks at me, the way he talks with me when we're not being dirty . . . even the fact that he spent hours last night hanging out while I helped Elise through her latest drama and did so without a single complaint.

Derrick . . . God, he's everything I could ask for, so hot I find myself thinking of him and wondering if I could run to the bathroom at work to send him a quick naughty video. And he's intelligent and perceptive, and even gentlemanly in a lot of ways. If telling a woman you want to fuck her until she passes out from so many orgasms can be called gentlemanly, Derrick's figured out how.

But that's what's scaring the shit out of me . . . every high has to be met with an equal low. Locking a forced excitement to my face, I tell my mom the same thing I told Jessie about it being our second date but we've been talking for a few weeks. "Really, it's no big deal."

Mom rolls her eyes, refusing to be put off. "No big deal? This is so exciting! New potential, new stories, the anticipation of liking each other and falling in love."

She hugs me, forgetting her earlier concerns about getting makeup on her wedding gown, and I just smile and nod back. Maybe Mom is getting her big island of happiness again, but I'm still last week's floating Styrofoam cup. "Yeah, we'll see."

CHAPTER 13

"*I* really think tonight's sponsor should be ChapStick or something," I joke, glancing again at the pre-show sheet. "I mean . . . blowjobs? They actually approved that one?"

"Well, there were a few requirements," Susannah says, smiling. She's been a lot nicer today than the past couple of days. I dunno, maybe whatever was biting her ass has worked itself out, or maybe she just realized that being pissed wasn't doing us any favors.

"What's that?" I ask, sipping my water and already thinking to tonight. Kat . . . blowjobs . . . Kat's blowjobs . . . fuck, I'm hard again. "Sorry, one more time?"

"I said, they want us to do a series of shows on oral sex," Susannah says, looking at her clipboard.

I groan. "Sounds like we're going to be fielding a lot of callers to fill all that time."

"We'll make it work like usual," she replies. "You ready?"

"Five minutes," I reply. "Just want to make sure . . . well, no early bathroom breaks."

I rush to the bathroom, pulling my phone out of my pocket as soon as I'm in the stall. *Thinking of u.*

Oh? What's tonight's show?

I smirk, wondering if I should tell the truth or not. *You'll just have to listen and find out. See you tonight.*

I do try to force out whatever's inside, but no dice. Still, I flush and get to the studio just in time to plop down in my chair. The entry music starts, and I lean into my mic just as Suz gives me a thumbs-up. "Good evening, listeners! This is Derrick King, the Love Whisperer, welcoming you to the next three hours of advice, music, and a little bit of fun. With me, of course, is my right-hand woman, Susannah 'Don't Call Her Jenna' Jameson."

"Tonight's show is about a subject that, well, let's just say it's near and dear to my heart."

"I didn't know your heart was next to your balls," Susannah jokes, and I have to grin. That was a good one.

"Well, let's just say I've thought about this subject a lot. You want the honor of telling our audience what we'll be discussing?"

"Sure, D. Tonight, let's talk fellatio. Blowjobs, knob slobbing, or sucking cock. Take your pick. If it involves dicks and lips, we're gonna talk about it tonight."

"Hell of an intro. I always liked the term *blowjob* myself," I admit. "By the way, if blowjobs aren't your thing, don't worry, folks, we're having a show on licking pussy too. But for now, you know the deal. Give us a call, drop us an email. The lines are open. First, let's go to an email. Suz, will you start us off?"

"Love to," Susannah says, lowering her voice to a sultry purr to set the tone. She's got a great range of voices, from shrill to sexy. I guess that's why she's working in this business. "Dear Love Whisperer, I've got a problem. You see, my boyfriend wants me to blow him, but I struggle with it. Am I doing it right? Is he gonna choke me? What about when he comes . . . what do I do? His birthday is coming up, and I'd love to give him this gift. See if I can make it happen for him. Advice? From Kitty."

Kitty? Great, just fucking awesome. I'm trying to work, and all I can think of is Kat crawling across the floor like a kitten, her lips stretched wide around my cock, balls-deep in her mouth. Shit. Focus. I gotta be a pro here. "Well, Kitty," I husk, licking my lips before I can continue, "first, I'd like to say you're quite the girlfriend if you're worried about this. For a lot of guys, blowjobs tend to consist of a little begging, some half-hearted licks, and then it's time to move on."

"Not me," Susannah teases, and I give her a raised eyebrow. She normally doesn't get this expressive. Maybe she's just really into it tonight. "I love feeling my man slide over my tongue."

"That's the thing," I add. "Kitty, there are two main ingredients to a good blowjob. One, you have to really devote yourself to it. Don't just do it because you think he'll like it. You have to suck him off because you *want* to. Show some excitement about it because it's supposed to be sexy and fun! Second, pay attention to what he likes. Does he want it hard, lots of tongue action, deep-throating, hands involved, or not involved? Maybe some ball play or even a little bit of anal play. Pay attention to what he likes, and then when you find out, give it to him and don't hold back."

"So, Derrick, what do you like?" Susannah asks, a gossipy tone to her voice. "I'm sure our listeners would love to know your hottest desires . . . fast and rough, teasing little sucks, maybe the grapefruit trick I've been hearing about?"

I purse my lips, thinking, and all I can see is Kat. My cock throbs in my pants, and I smirk before answering. "I'm gonna be honest, I'm not sure there's such a thing as a bad blowjob. Unless there's teeth," I say, a shudder of fear snaking through my body. "But I'm sure some guys are into that too. But I'd advise a Q-and-A before going that route, ladies. But let's just say that I'm loving what I'm getting."

"Oh, *he* must be good then," Susannah shoots back, a little cattier than I expected, but before I can say anything, she gives a big laugh. "All right, let's try a caller. Go ahead, Eric."

I don't have time to ask Suz what the fuck was up with that crack because I've gotta help this caller. *"Yeah, uh, first thing, big fan, Derrick. You've helped me a lot with my girl. Big props to you."*

"Thanks, Eric. What can I help you with tonight?"

"Well, how can I convince my girl that swallowing isn't deadly? I swear, every time she goes down on me it's either she pulls off in time for me to blow on her face or she starts spitting like a garden sprinkler. But I really, really want to see her take a mouthful and swallow it down, know what I mean?"

"I do. It's a pretty common thing for a lot of guys," I reply, trying to pull my thoughts together. "At the same time, a lot of women don't like it. Some of it is cultural or demographic. They've been taught that cum is somehow dirty or gross. Spitting can feel like they're rejecting you on some level, and swallowing seems sexy, like they're taking a part of you into themselves." I pause. Susannah raises a hand at me, and I segue to include her. "Susannah, what's your take?"

She smiles, her eyes glinting with naughtiness. "So many thoughts. From the woman's perspective, there's a point of gag where nothing's going to stop your body's natural reaction. The trick is to get behind the gag or in front of it. She needs to take you deeper down her throat so that when you come, it goes down easier. Or, maybe compromise and stay in front of the gag, come into her open mouth, get the visual of her with a mouthful and then she swallows like a good girl without the pressure of you continuing to fuck her face at the same time."

"Good advice. Thanks for the female point of view. Also, Eric . . . man-to-man here, this might not be about her. Are you making it attractive for her to want to put her face in your crotch? I mean, what's your lifestyle like?"

"Uhm, I'm pretty busy. I work long hours but do my best to stay healthy. I take vitamins, stuff like that."

"All good, but before you want to get down with your lady, make sure you're showered and fresh, and stay hydrated," I reply. "And lay off alcohol and caffeine, and if you do smoke . . . well, this is another reason to quit. Eat right too. All of these things have been shown to affect the taste of your cum. Keep it clean, keep it healthy, and hopefully, tasty."

We continue, and I give Eric a few pointers. Once we're done, it's time for a music break, so I turn it over to Susannah, who spins Madonna's 'Like a Prayer.'

"Little old-school, isn't it?" I ask once the mics are off. She gives me a look, and there's something different about the way she's looking at me. Back to that upset look, I don't know.

"Best song about blowjobs ever made," Susannah says before singing along with some of the lyrics. I raise my eyebrow. She's got a point, but I've got other things on my mind.

Leaving the booth, I pull out my phone, texting Kat. *You listening?*

Of course. And no, I'm not Kitty, just in case you were wondering. I know just how to make you come in my mouth. And don't worry, it's delicious.

I moan, thinking of the sight of her and text back. *I wish I could see you naked and with my dick in your mouth right now.*

Well, we'll see if I can make that happen later.

I hear the song wrapping up, so I hop back in the booth while Susannah grumbles, "We've got work to do."

"Chill, Suz, we've got this," I reply. Madonna finishes up her ode to the sacrilegious blowjob, and we go to an email about a woman who gets off most when she's got her head tilted back off the edge of the bed. The idea's hot, though I've never tried it. I toss it to Susannah. "I dunno, Suz, sounds like a good way to get a head rush for the sucker, not the suckee."

She laughs a little. "Maybe some people like a little head rush? For real, don't hang upside down too long. This is a finishing move that will get you past your gag reflex like we talked about earlier with Eric. But don't go falling off the bed and blaming your concussion on us."

We bounce back and forth, taking calls and doing music breaks for the next hour. I try to stay focused on my job, but about halfway through, I get another buzz on my cell-phone. Dad.

How is the show going tonight, Derrick?

That's Dad, never uses a single text contraction or emoji or anything. *Not bad. Hey, Jacob will be at home to play in a few weeks and got us box tickets. Can you go?*

Of course I can go. It's football so I'll be watching either way, there or at the house.

Growing up, that was what he and I bonded over first. Not that he didn't let me explore other things, but where some fathers would tell their son about the baseball greats or take their sons camping, with us, it was football. Oh, we'd still go fishing or hiking, but his 'old man stories' weren't about fish that got away but about watching Dwight Clark make 'The Catch,' or Doug Flutie's miracle throw while at Boston College. We bonded over the somehow fated Super Bowl win of the Patriots after 9/11, and now that my former college roommate is a pro and relatively local . . . well, Dad's got a reason to closely follow the team.

I know he felt like it was the end of an era when I quit playing, but ultimately, I think he's glad I did reporting. Especially with all the medical data these days about players getting their heads smacked on the field. Now, I think he's still trying to understand just what this whole Love Whisperer thing is about. Personally, I'm glad he's probably not listening in tonight. Better for him to think I talk about love and relationships than blowjobs and swallowing.

OK, I text him. *I'll send you details tomorrow. Jacob should have them to me by then.*

"Yo, Derrick!" Susannah growls, and I look up guiltily. "We've got a show to do!"

"My bad," I reply, setting my phone down on the table. The light comes on saying we're live. "We're back, and I hope you've been drinking plenty of water, because it's getting warm in here. What do we have next, Susannah?"

"A little offshoot from the norm," she says, grinning wickedly. "We've got Jamie, who has one of my personal fantasies happening in real life."

"Go ahead, Jamie, I'm listening."

"Hi, Derrick," a woman says. *"I've just started a new relationship with a guy from France, and he's had a lot more experience than me. Last Friday night, I came home and he . . . well, he was on his knees with another man. They invited me to join in, and while the sex was mind-blowing, I'm a little worried in that my boyfriend seems to be more into sucking cock himself than into me. He's asked if he could invite his friend over again this weekend, and I'm not sure what to say."*

Well, now, that's awkward. I get through the call with the same advice I normally give, communicate and be honest with each other, because what the fuck else can I really say to that? But by the time we're done, it's time for another commercial break. As soon as the clear light goes on, I reach for my phone, tapping out a message to Kat.

1 hr left.

U can do it!

I smirk, naughty thoughts running through my head. *Got anything to motivate me?*

I seriously don't expect her to reply, and at first I think maybe she's busy. With about thirty seconds left in the commercial break, my phone buzzes again and I pick it up to see it's a pic.

"Oh, Jesus," I whisper as I see Kat, naked from the waist up, her hair framing her face as she shows me a mouthful of what's obviously milk or something, but the image gets through, especially as she's let a little dribble from the side of her mouth.

Motivated enough?

I gulp, my cock surging in my pants until I'm nearly desperate to have some relief. With shaking thumbs, I text back. *Don't plan on sleeping alone. And no panties 4 our date.*

She sends back an evil smiley emoji, and I've got a very horny and very worried feeling that I've unleashed a long-repressed . . . perfection.

So what is a second date to you?

Kat's quick with her reply. *It's late, so pick me up. We can have drinks at a bar around the corner.*

I'm aware enough to see Susannah giving me the signal, and I go back to the show, faking my way through another email. As soon as I can, I'm back on my phone with Kat.

Still listening?

Always. Getting some new ideas too. If you're good . . . maybe I'll show you. Not second date tho. Gotta wait a little longer.

My balls are aching, but her message is clear. No sex tonight. Fuck. Okay, I guess I'll survive. I try to go back to the show, but I'm distracted by thoughts of Kat and I know I'm fumbling my way through some of the calls. Hopefully, no one's noticing.

During the next song break, Fifty's *Candy Shop*, I duck out to not only take a piss but to get my head right.

Honestly, Suz does have a reason to be upset with me. I realize I've phoned it in tonight, on exactly the type of show I shouldn't be. God, just the idea of three hours of talk about blowjobs has me rolling my eyes while at the same time, my cock pulses in my pants, thinking of Kat and her pic.

But that's the problem, I should be focusing, I should be able to for three hours. I shouldn't be focusing on Kat but instead on each of my callers. If I get bored, I crack jokes with Susannah about the calls or emails. I deliver on the mic, not on text.

"Tomorrow," I promise myself as I head back down the hallway. I open the door to see Susannah not in her mini-booth but in mine. Surprised, I stop to see her set my phone down on my desk. "Somethin' wrong?"

"Sorry," she says, seemingly all smiles. "Your phone was buzzing around again. I turned it off for now, if you don't mind. We really need to focus and finish tonight out right."

"I agree," I reply a little sheepishly. "I'm sorry about tonight's show. I know it's been a clusterfuck sometimes, and you've saved my ass. I'll do better tomorrow."

"I get it, I really do," Susannah says. "Derrick, we've all got shows that are tough and lives outside this place. But we've got the potential to do really great things here, bigger and better than ever, but that will never happen if you're fucking around, barely dialing it in for the shows. I'm happy to do the prep, research, and planning. All you've got to do is show up and speak, but tonight, you've barely done that. I need you to be a fucking pro like usual, okay?"

The venom in her last sentence irks me and I'm about to

shoot back about her own cattiness, but Fifty's ending and we've got to get back on the air.

Somehow, we get through the rest of the show and ironically, things go well enough that as the outro music plays, Susannah's in a lot better mood. "Hey, D?"

I'm in a hurry to see Kat, but still, I look over, leaning back in my chair. "Yeah?"

"Sorry about the bitch act before. I'm just worried about you, that's all. Is everything okay? You keep texting and calling and that's not you. This isn't the first time that's happened lately either. You seem distracted. Anything I can do to help?"

I shake my head, getting out of my chair. "No, I'll get it together. I'm sorry too. Do me a favor though—let's just keep this between us, but I met someone and it's a little all-consuming. I got this, promise."

"Fresh relationships are like that," Susannah agrees. "Lucky girl. Is that all?"

"No, I was talking to my dad but he's fine. Just been awhile since I really spent time with him, so I gave him some more text time than I should have. All good, sorry if I wasn't pulling my weight. I'll do better."

"Okay," Susannah says, giving me her trademark smile. "Keep it up though, and I'll make sure that we do a whole slew of topics that you hate. Should I go crazy romantic until you vomit pink roses, or some seriously kinky fetish that makes your ass pucker? I got it . . . baby talk. Does Derrick-werrick need a little powder-poofy?" She laughs maniacally, and I can't help but grin at her. This is why we work together.

"Okay, okay . . . I promise to get it together as long as you never, ever call me *that* again! You mind wrapping up the studio? I kinda have a date." I smile, knowing it's a big ask after the night we've had but hopeful she'll cut me some slack because I need to get to Kat.

"Go party, Don Juan de Radio," Suz says. "But I demand perfection tomorrow. We're poised for great things!"

I'm already walking toward the door, thankful for the reprieve, but I answer her. "We *are* doing great things, Suz. We're actually helping people here."

She says it softly, but I hear it anyway. "But we could help more if we had a bigger platform. Syndication, Derrick. We're so close."

"It'll happen or it won't, Suz. I'm happy either way. Don't worry about chickens that aren't even eggs yet. Anyway, gotta run. Thanks! You're the best. Tomorrow . . . I promise. I'm back on track and ready to rock." And before the door even closes behind me, all thoughts of work whoosh out of my head to be replaced with Kat and how she's waiting for me.

CHAPTER 14

"Well, well, this isn't too bad," Derrick says as he closes the door to the bar behind me, cutting off the icy wind. The holiday season isn't that far off, and honestly, I'm making a few early Christmas wishes even if I know they won't come true.

"It's no dive, but it's not so fancy that nobody can afford a mineral water," I admit. "As long as you don't mind not having a coat check girl."

"Never had a need for that," Derrick growls, looking me over. "I've got everything I want right here."

Heat creeps up my neck as he consumes me with his gaze, and I know that I made the right choice in clothes. Sure, my calves are cold, but this hip hugging skirt and tight blouse look sexy as hell. Or at least it seems to tick all the boxes that Derrick likes.

"Should we sit?" I ask, and Derrick nods, his hand warm on my lower back as he leads me over to a corner table.

The lights are low. It's that time of night where people are here to either quietly drink their sorrows away or find someone.

"You know," Derrick says as he takes my jacket to hang it over one of the spare chairs, "you didn't have to."

"Didn't have to what?" I ask, waiting while the waitress comes over. I order a glass of white wine while Derrick orders a beer on tap, and we decide on some tapas to give us something to nibble on besides each other.

"You didn't have to get dressed up," Derrick says. "You don't need to show off for me. I feel like you've never been more comfortable than when we hung out over breakfast and you were wearing yoga pants and an old white t-shirt."

"I'm trying to be more comfortable," I admit. "But no way am I going out with you wearing *that*."

Derrick smiles and nods. "Just so you know. You're sexy, beautiful, *and* you've got brains. What's there not to like?"

"Good question," I reply. "What about you? You've gotta have a few bad tendencies."

"Sure," Derrick says, pausing when our drinks are brought and we toast each other. "For one, I'm terrible at laundry. In fact, I've got a single method. I pick up everything on the floor and chuck it all in the washer at once. Main reason I have all dark clothes . . . black, grey, charcoal, navy."

"You what?" I ask, sipping my wine. It's good and warm as it flows down my throat.

"Let's just say . . . pink football practice pants," Derrick says with a chuckle. "Take one pair of football pants, two brand-new red cotton t-shirts, throw in hot water with cheap detergent, and magic happens. So yeah, all darks and that doesn't happen."

I laugh, imagining Derrick wearing pink football pants. "Okay, that'll teach you. Thankfully for me, wearing pink pants isn't a problem."

"Nope, never had a problem with you and anything pink," Derrick purrs, heat blooming between my legs. "So . . . how was your day? Miss me?"

I giggle, thinking of all that we've done so far today. "How could I have? You were texting me all day."

"When I get motivation like you sent me, I have to."

"I admit, that was pretty dirty. I hope you didn't get in trouble."

"Not too much. Susannah did almost kill me today between texting you and my dad, but that's not your fault."

"Is he okay?" I ask, worried, and Derrick waves me off.

"Yeah, he was just checking in. I think he didn't realize the time at first. He knows I work in the studio, even if he doesn't listen in often . . . thankfully."

"Oh, I'm sure," I tease. "I mean, what father would want to listen to their son talk all about how to please a man with your mouth? Speaking of which . . . you never answered some questions tonight about what you like best."

Derrick leans in, smiling. "I think you know the answer to that one. You know exactly what I like. And for a woman who said that she wasn't going to do it anyway, you're waving a red flag at a bull that's about to charge you."

"Don't let me taunt you at work. I know how serious you take helping your listeners. After all, look where we are," I joke back, my pussy tingling underneath my skirt. "You've helped me a lot so far."

Derrick nods, reaching across the table to place his warm fingers on top of my hand, sparks radiating up my arm from the contact. "I take it very seriously. What can I do to keep helping you, Kitty Kat?"

There's a thousand things Derrick could do, but as we've moved into something more fragile here with actually dating, I know the most important thing he can do. "Maybe just show me a good time and that not all guys are after one thing?"

"And what one thing is that?"

"You know . . ." I whisper back, heat creeping up my neck again. "Fucking."

Derrick leans in closer, his voice low and seductive. "But what if I do want to fuck you? Right now, as much as I know I should be, I don't want to be a gentleman. I want to bend you over this table and slip your skirt over your ass. I could make you come right here."

I'd let you and come like a freight train, I think, but I have to keep control somehow, so I flirt back instead. "Rather public, don't you think?"

Derrick glances around, then comes back to me, his eyes burning. "Would you rather disappear to the back? We could do that if you want? Kat, I respect you and if you say no, I'll accept that. But . . . I think you want to say yes."

My breath catches in my chest. He's got me. Sure, I don't want to be easy to get, but the way he makes me feel, I want him inside me every fucking moment we're together.

Derrick leans in, his thumb drawing circles on my hand, making my nipples tighten in my bra and my pussy clench. "There's nothing wrong with wanting it. I want you just as much. We could sneak back there and find a dark corner, maybe you sink down to your knees and suck my cock right there. I'd stand in front of you so no one could see. No one would be the wiser but us. Only we would know how much you drive me crazy."

"I drive *you* crazy?" I murmur, feeling a little bit of control return. He's right, we both want it . . . we just have to figure out where. "Little ol' me?"

Derrick leans in closer, and our lips are this close to touching when there's a harsh harrumph next to us and a sneering laugh. I'm horrified to see Kevin standing there, smirking like he's busting me doing something wrong.

He looks a little extra swollen, obviously using his free time in the gym the last few weeks. And like super tan . . . orange fake-bake tan. Eww. I sit back, my elbow bumping my wine glass, but I catch it before it crashes to the floor. I definitely don't need any more attention in this moment. "Kevin? What the fuck?"

Kevin chuckles. "Seriously, Kat, this is sad. I mean this guy? He looks like a total douchebag."

"Fuck you!" I hiss, feeling the flush paint my cheeks. Deep down, I don't really care what Kevin thinks or says, but in the moment, with him sneering at me, it's hard not to react or to fall into old habits. "You don't get a say in whom I see. You cheated on me, remember?"

"Didn't take you long to find some new dick," Kevin replies, not taking the obvious hint to leave. He looks at Derrick, who's coiled tight, ready to get up if need be, but he's also letting me handle this myself for now. I appreciate that he knows I need to do this. He talks to Derrick, but Kevin's eyes are on me, watching his barbs hit home. "Can I give you a tip, man? You don't need to go through that much effort. She's an easy fuck. Not that good, but easy." He leans back, the pride at seeing the insecurities he's brought up in me obvious in his eyes.

Derrick's heard enough and gets to his feet. For the first time, I see that he actually towers over Kevin by a couple of inches.

"Okay, that's it," Derrick rumbles. "I've heard enough of this."

"Oh, I'm shaking in my boots," Kevin drawls, wiggling his fingers. "Why don't you sit back down, buddy? You don't know who you're talking to."

"Sure I do," Derrick says, his voice dropping to a threatening whisper. "You're the two-pump chump piece of shit who couldn't give Kat what she deserved. You took advantage of her, fucked around on her, and lost her.

Now, you've probably figured out that she was the best damn woman to walk into your life and you blew it. She figured out you're worthless, and she deserves better."

"And you think *you're* better?" Kevin says. He laughs, half turning away, but it's a feint. His left hand flashes out, catching Derrick just above the eyebrow, and the fight's on.

It's the first fight I've seen since a little push-shove thing in high school, and it's nothing like the movies. Nobody gets involved to peel them apart, but at the same time, it doesn't last long. Kevin tries to follow up his punch with another, but Derrick grabs his arm and somehow pushes it across his body. Kevin's thrown off-balance, and as he stumbles past, Derrick picks him up in a massive bear hug before slamming him to the floor of the bar.

"That's enough!" the bartender yells. "Don't make me call the cops!"

"Call them. I'm pressing charges," Kevin whines from underneath Derrick. "He assaulted me."

"Boy, from where I'm sittin', you threw the first punch and he defended himself from your shenanigans. Where I come from, you put money in the register, you gon' get a receipt more often than not," one of the bar patrons drawls. "Figure at least four more of us saw the same thing."

Kevin looks like he's about to whine, but he slumps down. Derrick gets up, and I notice he's bleeding. I go to touch the wound as Kevin gets up, grabbing a tumbler off a nearby table, but one hard look from

Derrick is all it takes, and he lets go of the weapon to leave the bar.

"Are you okay?" Derrick asks, turning to look at me for the first time. "I'm sorry. I would have let you handle that, but he was being a bit too much of an asshole."

I feel oddly excited. I mean, Derrick just went Neanderthal. Why not clunk me on the head and drag me back to his cave by the hair? But I'm turned on, power coursing through me not only in that I stood up to Kevin, but that Derrick had my back.

I grab his head and pull him down into a deep kiss, our tongues swirling as I reward him for being there for me. "Let's get out of here and get that cut looked at," I whisper.

I usher Derrick onto the couch, where I strip off my jacket. "Okay, let me get the alcohol," I say, going to grab my kit.

I come back, soaking a few cotton balls in alcohol. I dab at his cut, which is a lot deeper than I expected. "Damn," Derrick says, inspecting it. "Got any tape?"

"Uh . . . probably," I say, looking in my kit. "Why?"

"Learned from a friend," Derrick says, taking the roll. He tears strips and carefully covers the cut with a narrow piece of gauze before taping his eyebrow back together. "Damn . . . could have done without this, but there was no way I was throwing the first punch."

"You let him hit you," I whisper, running my finger through his hair just above his eyebrow. "Why?"

"Because you deserve to have someone take a punch for you," Derrick says, his hand closing over mine and pulling me closer. "Besides, I heard somewhere that chicks dig scars."

I chuckle and gently trace my fingertips along his forehead and down around his eye to his cheek. I'm checking for any tender spots but mostly just marking him with my touch, appreciating that he was willing to sacrifice himself for me. I dip down, finding his lips with mine, hoping he feels the *thank you* I'm trying to communicate with my kisses. The fire we've been stoking for the last few days rages at my center, and I need to . . . worship him. This man isn't showing me who I am but is helping me actually discover who I am for myself, which feels even more important. I lower to my knees, my face level with the hardness already pressing against his jeans.

"Kat, you don't have to. What about our second date?" There's a plea to his voice, and I know he's trying his damndest to do the right thing. But I know that *this* is the right thing. It's not some guidebook dating rule, arbitrary so everyone thinks you're a 'good girl'. This is just real and what I want. Using all the tips from the show today, and maybe a few tricks of my own, I take Derrick to the edge in minutes.

"Damn it, Kat. Just like that . . . suck that cock, take me all in. Are you gonna swallow for me? Because I'm about to fill you up. Where do you want it?" I feel his balls pull tight, and I suck him in deep, leaving no doubt to my answer. I swallow down every drop, satisfaction humming through me.

I lay my head on his thigh, tracing lines along his softening cock as he pants above me. I realize that I'm really falling for him, despite my misgivings and fears, and that's both exciting and terrifying. He's not just healing my heart like the casual rebound I though this might be, but he's filling my heart with new hopes and dreams, which feels dangerous.

CHAPTER 15

DERRICK

*T*wake up in an increasingly familiar, comfortable tangle of arms and legs, opening my eyes to see again the increasingly familiar poster of Einstein with his tongue poking out that's next to the closet. I stretch, feeling Kat's breast shift to press warmly against my ribs. "Mmm, good morning."

"Mid-morning." Kat yawns sleepily. "You better be glad that my job lets me do flex time, stud. Let's get brunch."

I hum happily, turning over and kissing her forehead. "I don't know about brunch, but I've got a nice sausage for you if you're interested."

Kat chuckles but reaches down and gives my cock a good morning stroke. "I've never thought of myself as sexually insatiable before meeting you. Now it's like sex is as necessary as oxygen or high-speed Wi-Fi."

I laugh and give her a kiss. After the passionate heat of

last night, both of our bodies are taken care of for now, and we roll out of bed, getting ready for the day.

"How's the eye?" Kat asks as she quickly showers. "Oh, and if you don't mind pink, I've got some disposable razors in the medicine cabinet. Gonna have to use soap though."

"Conditioner will do the trick," I reply, finding a bottle and squeezing it out. "Did a show on grooming for love-making once and found out that conditioner is better for softening the hair and the skin than soap. As for the eye, not too bad. The tape held it together."

We swap places, and I wash carefully, avoiding my eye. When I get out, Kat's already in her bedroom getting dressed. What I see stirs both my loins and something else as she pulls on a pair of her ever-present jeans, but instead of one of her normal shirts, she has on one of mine. "Where'd you get that?"

"You left it the second night you came over," Kat says, blushing. It's adorable. My shirt practically swallows her to the point she could wear it like a dress if she wants. "Mind if I wear it?"

"Looks better on you than it ever did on me," I say, pulling her in close. "You're beautiful, Katrina Snow. And you make me feel lucky to be part of your life."

We kiss tenderly while I pick her up, amazed at how far things have gone and glad at the same time. I set her down, looking at the way my shirt covers her, wrapping her up the way I'd like to but knowing we need to get some food . . . fuel, whatever.

She steps back, putzing with the oversized shirt, rolling the sleeves and tying it at the waist in an almost country-girl fashion, but when she's done, I whistle. "Woman, you definitely make that shirt look better than I ever did. As far as I'm concerned, it's yours. And I want to see you in that and nothing else very soon."

Kat looks at herself in the mirror and gives me a grin. Reaching down, she unbuttons one more button, giving me a hint of her cleavage. "You make me feel sexy, and I want the world to know it. Now . . . pancakes!"

We drive to a nearby restaurant, ordering complete brunch specials, and chat innocently while sipping our orange juice. Just after our plates arrive, I hear a voice call out my name. "Hey, D!"

I turn, grinning as Jacob dominates the room, his massive presence almost making the tightly packed tables and booths melt away. "Jacob, I didn't even know you were in town."

"Yeah, well, team's got a long week with the Monday night game, so Coach gave us an extra day off. Who's your friend?" Jacob asks, giving Kat his Sports Illustrated megawatt smile. "Jacob Knight. Pleased to meet you."

"Jacob, this is my girlfriend, Katrina Snow. Kat, Jacob's my old college roommate."

His eyes widen a little at my calling Kat my girlfriend, and I didn't even mean to say it at first—it just sort of came out. But it feels right, and as the surprise melts away, I can see that Kat's pleased as punch with the designation.

"It's nice to meet you," Kat says. "Join us for brunch?"

"That little snack? We're in the middle of the season. I need protein, so excuse me . . ." He motions to the waitress, who buzzes to the table, seemingly overjoyed to be asked to come over judging by the way she's been eyeing Jacob. "Can I get a half-dozen eggs, scrambled, four slices of bacon, extra crispy, and a bowl of oatmeal with a touch of brown sugar?" The waitress nods absently in a trance as she stares at Jacob's mouth before she snaps out of it and scurries off. Jacob laughs, looking back at us. "What do you think the chances are she's going to get that right?"

He settles in, and under the table, I can feel Kat's hand rest on my thigh. She gives me a squeeze, and when I look in her eyes, they're full of emotion that I know we'll talk about soon.

For now, though, Jacob's full of energy and questions. "So, where'd you get the shiner, man? Didn't I teach you enough to avoid a beating?"

"It's not a shiner. It's a cut. And that deflection move that you and I drilled for two summers came in handy," I tell him. I fill him in on the incident with Kevin, Jacob's face clouding at first before clearing.

"So, he did you right?" Jacob asks Kat, who smiles and nods. "Good. Because if he doesn't, give me a call. I'll show him a few moves that I haven't taught him yet. I wouldn't worry, though. D's a good man."

I watch as Jacob and Kat get to know each other, and I'm glad to see that they get along well. They're total and complete opposites, the towering physical gladiator who makes his millions by terrorizing quarterbacks while she makes apps for smartphones and tablets, but it seems to be working. He's gregarious and rarely stops talking, asking questions and giving her quieter approach a direction to keep the conversation rolling.

"So, you listen to Derrick's show?" Kat asks in surprise. "Just didn't think that'd happen. You're sort of . . ."

"Big?" Jacob asks ironically, making Kat laugh. "Yeah, well, if anything, that helps guys like me. I ain't ashamed to admit it—I've used a few tips D's said to help things along. Haven't found the right girl yet, but that's okay. I gotta say, though," he says as he stares Derrick down. "You've never called me up after a breakup to see if I was doing okay." He fakes a sniffle, tracing a dry fingertip down his cheek like it's a tear before grinning madly.

I see Kat blush, and I know just what she's thinking about. "You're a big boy. I figure you know to pick up the phone if that's what you need. No offense."

"None taken," Jacob says. Kat gets up, and he rises like a gentleman. "You okay?"

"Yeah." Kat giggles, charmed. "Just two cups of coffee and then OJ . . . ladies' room is calling. Excuse me a moment."

Kat walks away, and Jacob turns back to me. "Seems like a good girl. She gets the stamp of approval."

I laugh. "Didn't know I needed one, but thanks. Why's that?"

"Just seems like the girl for you, that's all. Listen, D, I've known you for almost a decade now. Everyone has a type

165

that's meant for them. Me . . . I need some kick-ass chick who's going to take no prisoners and probably butt heads with me right up until the point we're tearing each other's clothes off. You though, you're the kind that needs someone you just gel with. And while you two aren't peas and carrots, you gel."

"Peas and carrots?" I ask, smirking. "Let me guess, *Forrest Gump* on the last cross-country flight?"

"Besides," Jacob continues, not getting thrown off at all, "you like her too. I can see it in your eyes and not just that cut over your eyebrow. She's doing something to you, man. And in my opinion, it's a *good* something."

"Yeah, well, I gotta take my time. The asshole ex we told you about isn't the only guy who's treated her like shit in the past. So I plan to just treat her right, go slow, and treat her with the respect that I don't think any other man has ever given her, and we'll see what happens."

Jacob nods sagely. "Well said, brother. Might not be a complex game plan, but it's a solid one. Hey, I can get you another ticket for the game if you want to bring her with your dad."

"Fuck, yeah!" I reply, grinning. "You're the best, man."

"I can get you one of the cheerleader outfits for her too . . . if the Love Whisperer is into that."

I close my eyes, imagining Kat in a cheerleader outfit. Not a bad idea, but maybe later. "Probably not a safe idea for now. But thanks for the offer."

CHAPTER 16

KAT

I feel giggly and light as I wrap up my coding for the evening, knowing that I'm rocking this new app and am right on target for my deadline. I kick back in my cubicle, pulling out my phone. "I can miss Derrick's show for *one* night," I say to myself. "Besides, I can get the real deal any time I want now. So . . ."

I hit speed dial, glad that I have most of the office to myself.

After just two rings, the call's picked up. "Hey, babe, how's life in the silicon world?"

I smile. Sounds like Elise is doing better. "Not bad, how's life in the dirt sheets?"

"Same as always, dirty, and I can only tell half of it," Elise says. "Gimme some good news. I can use some after the shit I listened to today."

"Well . . ." I say, drawing it out, "you won't believe what happened last night."

I tell Elise about my night out that turned into a night of passion with Derrick, leaving out my nude 'swallow' pic, glossing over most of my day and really starting the story after Derrick picked me up and we went to the bar.

"That local place we've been to?" Elise asks. "Fancy."

I chuckle at the sarcasm and continue. "Derrick didn't mind. Actually, it was going great. We'd gotten our tapas order in and were sharing more about ourselves. Derrick was flirting with me pretty hardcore, but I liked it."

"You seem to like everything he does," Elise says, but there's not too much jealousy there. "At least tell me he's hung like a peanut so I don't have to kill you."

"Sorry, you're just gonna have to kill me," I joke back. "But, you'll love him too when you hear what happened next. Kevin showed up."

"That son of a bitch," Elise growls. "Bastard better be glad I wasn't there. I'd have castrated him with a broken beer bottle."

I don't doubt it, and that's why I love her so damn much. "Derrick wasn't too happy either. But he was so fucking awesome. First, he let me handle it, just having my back. But when Kevin crossed the line . . . Derrick handed him his ass."

"Is that so?" Elise comments, impressed. "Well then, babe, I'm starting to like Derrick more and more. Anyone who stands up for my girl is worth a thank you grope."

"Uh-huh, hands off my man. This morning, we went to brunch and he introduced me to Jacob Knight . . . as his girlfriend."

"Jacob Knight, the football stud?" Elise says, whistling. "Phew, that's a lot of man there. I've heard rumors about him too. Let's just say the man knows his way around the field, in football and with women."

"Maybe, but he was a total gentleman with me. As we were leaving, he even said he'd get me a ticket to join Derrick and his father for an upcoming game. I'm . . .I can't believe I'm saying this, but I'm excited to go to a football game!"

"Sounds like you'd be excited to go to a demolition derby if it was with Derrick," Elise says. "Maybe he can use that sexy radio voice to tell you all the plays step by detailed step." She mimics a sultry seductress tone. "The tight end grabs the ball, tugging it close to his body and letting loose a burst of speed as he thrusts toward the end zone. Touchdown. Oh, my . . . the celebratory champagne seems to have spilled all over his sweaty body. Bubbles popping . . . everywhere."

I erupt into giggles at her silly antics. "Holy shit, Elise. That's some upper-level imagination there, and I didn't know you had that voice. You never told me you were a phone-sex operator, but I'd believe it now. Were you undercover for a story or just needing a bit of extra cash?"

She laughs back, taking my teasing in stride. "Whatever. You try that voice on Derrick and he'll be eating out of your hand . . . or whatever orifice you want him to eat out." We're both quiet for a moment, the laughter giving way but the smile still stretching my face. "But seriously, babe, if I didn't know any better . . ."

"What?" I ask, curious where she's going now after her little tangent.

"Nothing, it's just . . . what do you feel for him? What's happening with you two?"

I bite my lip, chewing thoughtfully as I try to figure out the words. "Elise, since getting together with Derrick, I feel like a little bit of that darkness inside me is starting to fade. He's a gentleman with a naughty streak a mile wide that he still respects me with. He's protective, he's kind, he listens when I bore the shit out of him talking about work . . . I think I'm falling for him. Hard."

"Whoa. You sure, babe? I mean, I'm happy as fuck for you, but . . . you're you. And no offense, but this sounds awfully fast. I mean, considering what you've been through."

"I know, which is part of what scares the hell out of me. There's no logic in this, and I need a balanced pro/con sheet to feel like life makes sense. He's a radio personality with a sports background. I'm going to be reading *Football For Dummies* so I can understand the damn game I'm invited to. He's tall and built like a Greek statue. I'm . . . well, like you said, I'm me."

"So you're scared," Elise says. "You're going by your guts and not your brains."

"And you know what happens when I let my heart get

involved," I reply. "What if D's just like every other man I've let inside?"

"He could be, but he could also be the guy who might give you what you most deserve," Elise says. "A happily ever after."

"A happily ever after? Those are for cheesy romance books and fairy tales."

Elise snickers and raises her voice, singing, *"When you wish upon a star . . ."*

"Yeah, yeah," I snort. "You're a horrible Jiminy Cricket. No offense, but your conscience is not much better than mine, and you're a hell of a lot hotter."

"Why, thank you. I do say I'm a lot more fuckable than an insect," Elise retorts. "Listen, I gotta ask up front after your Kevin bombshell, or lack of bombshelling, I should say. Does Derrick knock your socks off?"

I giggle, feeling warmth between my thighs as I think of Derrick last night. "My socks, my panties, my bra . . . he's the best *ever*. If he were a computer program, he'd be the Big Oh-S-E-X."

"Apple's so going to love that you're making fun of their operating system." Elise snickers. "Nerd dirty talk, gotta love it. So, what's his style? Pound you into submissive bliss, or do you like to take charge?"

"That's the thing," I admit, my heart beating a little faster, "he's so good at listening, reading my body language. Like last night, I started off saying I wanted to be all prim and proper, no sex on the second date. But he read me so well and pushed his flirting to delicious naughtiness. My God, Elise, I was so ready to go to a dark corner and get it on in public. Me! In public! Can you imagine? But this morning, after we woke up, he totally saw that I wasn't really feeling it for sex, and we just talked as I showered. We even broke the toilet barrier."

"You're fucking shitting me," Elise says wonderingly. She's the one who introduced me to the various barriers, with the toilet barrier, or feeling comfortable enough to use the toilet in front of the other person, being one of the greatest. "You aren't *maybe* falling for him. You're head over heels for this guy. Is there any limit you won't cross with him?"

"I don't know. Sometimes, I feel like if that man asks me anything, I'd do it," I admit. "God, I can't believe it. I am so head over heels for this man. Okay, pause button pressed or I'm gonna get too worked up and have to call him back for a repeat performance." I shake my head a bit, rattling the sexy thoughts of Derrick out, and hear Elise laughing at me across the line. "What about you? Tell me about your day. Any better news about your boss? Are you still dating that same guy? The chef."

"Trevor?" Elise asks, snorting. "Nah, he was a tumbling, bumbling dickweed. Today's mostly sucked because I'm chasing some stupid celeb rumors. Fuck, why couldn't I have been on the Prince Harry and Meghan Markle beat?"

"Because you're barred from the UK after that little incident five years ago?" I tease, making Elise give me a long, loud raspberry in my ear.

"I wasn't banned from the whole country, just the Defence Ministry," Elise says. "And besides, the reporter's not going to England. It's all stateside reporting. I didn't get the assignment though because I'm not willing to fuck my way into plum assignments, unlike some people in my office," she says with a snotty tone. "Really, though, I'm cool. Standard stuff, nothing too exciting right now . . . usual celeb sightings, gossip mongering, ass-kissing, and covering to prevent lawsuits. Hey, what do you think of money shots?"

"Money shots?" I ask.

"Oh, come on, Kat. You know what a money shot is. When a guy blows his load all over—"

"I know what a money shot is. That was just so random I figured you meant something else."

Elise laughs. "Sorry, I'm chasing a rumor that there's a TV star whose specialty is getting money shots with some pretty A-list celebs. Can't name names yet, you know how that shit is, but what do you think?"

"I guess it depends on the couple? I mean, if they're both into it, who am I to say no?"

"Yup, you've been Love Whispered," Elise jokes. "So sweet, yet sexy, and no smut to you at all."

"You mean, too high-class," I tease. "Like you, babe. Elise, you're a legit journalist. I've read your real work. Why are you chasing down who blows a load in who's face?"

"Pays the bills for now. You know that. Just like your work

on that never-to-be mentioned again adult dating sim. Not saying I always like it, but it does pay well."

"Yeah, but . . ." I reply, then sigh, not wanting to make her feel bad about her job, even if she really is too good for the drivel she reports on. "Okay, I get it. So, now that Trevor's out of the way, anything interesting for you?"

"Not really, but I am hitting a club tonight with a few coworkers. It's *mostly* a work outing though. I won't be there looking to get my freak on," Elise admits. "Wanna join us? I got a new skirt that would make your ass look like a million bucks."

I think about it, then hum. "No can do. I got a man."

"What's your man got to do with me?" Elise asks, joking right along with me. "Come on, be my wing girl. I'm not going to get my freak on, but I didn't say I'm not gonna flirt. Drinks are on me."

I shake my head, leaning back. "No, that's okay, Elise. Not saying I'm not interested in hanging with my best friend . . . I'm just sort of hoping to see or talk to Derrick after his show, know what I mean?"

"I know exactly what you mean. Four letter word, starts with L, ends with E. You know, I . . ." Elise says, her words failing her for a moment. "I'm happy for you, Kat. I really am. Listen, I need to maintain my saucy bitchiness, so I'm gonna get ready to go. This weekend or something, girl time though, okay?"

"Only if you bring chocolate chip cookies to my place.

And you can teach me about football. You dated a quarterback in college, right?"

Elise laughs. "I caught more balls from him than anyone on the team, but that doesn't mean I know a damn thing about football. But we'll figure it out together. Talk to you later."

CHAPTER 17

DERRICK

*M*y phone is out of my pocket as soon as my front door's closed, and I flop down in my favorite chair, the line ringing in my ear.

"Hey, sexy man," Kat purrs, making my cock twitch. "I thought I heard a little tension in your voice tonight. What, behaving while you talked about how to go down on a woman for three hours has you worked up?"

I reach down, massaging my already hardening cock. "Fuck, Kitty Kat, you know I was thinking of you all show long. You were right to have your phone turned off. But . . . goddamn, I couldn't stop thinking of how good you taste."

"Mmm, I was thinking of you too. Especially when you talked about doing that figure-eight with your tongue, you naughty man, giving away your special move on me. Millions of women will thank you later."

"Just need one," I rasp, my cock hard and tenting my

pants. "Fuck, I miss you. Remind me again why we couldn't get together tonight?"

Kat chuckles, lowering her voice just the way she knows I like it. "Because *I* have to put in a *very* long, *hard* day behind my keyboard tomorrow," she teases. "*Someone's* been keeping me so distracted with thoughts of his big cock pumping in and out of me that I've got a lot to catch up on."

"You know I'm sorry about that," I half tease. "I thought I was inspiring you."

"Oh, you are, but if we saw each other tonight, we both know we're not going to get any sleep. I'd spend all night with my legs wrapped around your hips, pulling you into me and holding you deep inside."

"And that's a problem why?" I tease, reaching for the button on my jeans.

"Because I have to put the finishing touches on this app for the presentation at the end of the week. You know how hard I've been working on this. Other than being with you, I've put nearly every minute of every day for the last few months into this and it's all coming down to the presentation. I've got to prove myself as more than a one-hit wonder and the graphics are giving the team a hard time to integrate with the gesture-sensing technology . . . oops, sorry, I get a little excited and fall down the rabbit hole sometimes. It's just a few days apart and then we can have our next date at the football game."

I run my hand through my hair, knowing she's right but also knowing that I have to have her. "I know, I just miss you. Your business doesn't mean we can't go back to our roots a bit though, does it?"

There's a throaty, sexy chuckle that makes my throat go dry, and Kat comes back on. "Definitely not. But promise me one thing . . . one and done. This can't be an all-nighter."

One and done? The way I'm feeling right now, it might be five minutes and goodnight, but I'll do my best. "I promise."

My phone dings, and I see she's sending me a FaceTime call. I quickly hit the *Accept* button, and what I see makes my jaw drop.

Kat's grinning at me, already changed into a set of not trashy but definitely sexy lingerie, a sheer teddy and lacy boy shorts that give me quite a view of her ass cheeks as she poses, twirling for me before sitting down on her couch. "Whatcha think, boyfriend?"

"You little cock tease!" I growl even as I grin. "You had this planned all along."

"Maybe," Kat says with a naughty smirk. "Are you complaining?"

"Definitely not, just wish I were there with you to take that sexy top off with my teeth."

Kat giggles naughtily, running a thumb under the strap on her teddy. "Oh, this thing?" She plays with the straps on her shoulders, dipping them down in turn before pulling it back up and cupping her breasts, lifting them up for my inspection. "I just figured it showed off the feature you like best about me."

"You know I love your tits," I growl, leaning forward. "But I love every single thing about you. That's why I love you."

Kat stops, her eyes wide with emotion. We've said it to each other before, but it still hits with a lot of feeling every time. "And I love you. But . . ." she says, slipping back into her playful flirtiness, "I can't just pull my heart out of my chest. Things don't work that way. I can, however . . ."

Kat lifts her breasts up again, sliding the teddy down to reveal the beautiful half globes to me. Pressing them together, she jiggles them a little. "You do like these too, right?"

Reaching down off camera, I open my jeans, letting my cock jut out tall and stiff. "Yes, Kitty Kat, just like that. Show those perfect tits to me. Rub your thumb across your nipples until they're all pearled up for me."

Kat moans, doing just as I ask while lifting them. She tweaks and rubs her nipples, and I can't stop myself from reaching down to slowly stroke my cock. "Mmm, baby, I know you're amazing in person. But I won't lie, I've missed this. It's been awhile since we've had to do this long-distance, and it's . . ."

Her voice drifts off, and I add a bit of steel to my gravelly voice. "Tell me, Kat. Tell me what you're thinking, what you're feeling."

She lets out a sigh. "You make me feel clean and dirty at

the same time. I love imagining it's your hands squeezing me."

Kat tells me exactly how she feels, her hands massaging as she throws her head back, and my cock throbs in my grip. "Fuck you've got me so hard."

"Show me," Kat rasps, picking her phone up. "Show me that thick, beautiful cock that I love to feel stroking in and out of my soaked pussy."

I tilt my camera, showing her. I wrap my hand around my shaft, pumping it slowly until a drop of precum oozes out the top. "Is that what you like? You want that little raindrop, a bit of sweetness? I want to trace it along your lips like lipstick until you're glossy with it. And then have you lick it all off before you suck my cock to get more."

"Mmm," Kat moans. "You know I do. I love the taste of you. God, you make me feel so naughty."

"You're my naughty little slut now, aren't you?" I ask as I pump my cock for her, letting her see how the head swells with each stroke. "You dream of having my cock fucking you anywhere and everywhere you are."

"Oh, shit," Kat gasps. Her screen shifts, and I see that she's got two fingers buried inside her pussy already, pumping them in and out. "I love being your little plaything. Nothing boring about me now."

"Never was, you just needed to feel safe to explore." I moan, watching her fingers. "That's it, baby. Watch me, pace yourself with me. Slide those slick fingers into your tight little cunt as I fuck my fist for you." I time my strokes with her hand, both of us rising.

Kat cries out, needing more, and uses her other hand to tug her boy shorts the rest of the way down, lewdly spreading her legs and showing every sexy inch of herself to me. "Mmm . . . so, are you going to show me your pretty little asshole after the anal show?"

"Oh, God . . ." Kat whines, her fingers smearing her wetness around her clit before she plunges in again, her thumb stroking her clit. "I . . . I'd let you be my first. Fuck . . . oh, fuck, I'm gonna come soon."

"Do it, baby, I'm gonna come for you too," I reply, my hand speeding up. My cock throbs as I pump myself quickly, squeezing and relaxing. "My hand's not nearly as good as your hot, tight pussy, or even your little hands, but I could watch you tighten around your fingers, your thighs shaking forever. Squeeze your pussy tight, Kitty Kat. Choke those fingers the way I like it when you milk my cock." We both moan louder and louder, and it's enough. "Oh, fuck . . . Katrina!"

"Derrick . . ." Kat gasps as we both climax at the same time. I come hard, my cock erupting in thick spurts. Kat's hips shake and buck up and down on her couch, and it's a long time before either of us can move. When she does, she turns her phone to show me her smiling face. "Damn, baby . . . God, I love how you know just what to say."

"Just saying how you make me feel," I tell her. "And Kat . . . I love you."

She smiles, then giggles. "You love me all the way up to

your chest from the way it looks. Glad I make you wear a condom, or else you'd have come shooting out my nose."

I grab my discarded t-shirt, wiping off the mess a bit. We chat for about another thirty minutes until Kat yawns. "Ready to turn in?"

"I'm beat," Kat admits. "I just hate getting up to an alarm. You wake me up so much better."

"After your presentation Friday, I can wake you up just the way you like more and more often," I assure her. "Uhm . . . maybe this is too quick, but if you'd like, you can move some things over here. I've got space in my closet for you."

"The closet barrier, huh?" Kat says, giggling when I give her a confused look. "I'll explain later. Let me think on it, and I'll call you after work tomorrow. I love you, Derrick. G'night."

"G'night, Kat. I love you too."

CHAPTER 18

KAT

*I*t seems almost prophetic as I walk into the office, chugging what's already my second coffee of the day. It's Wednesday, and of course, the local radio station is cranking it loud. *I don't wanna work, I want to bang on the drum all day . . .*

"How nearly appropriate," I mutter to myself, half slinging my backpack onto my desk. Looking up, I see Tyler, one of the other coders. "Hey, Tyler, you mind turning that down?"

"Oh, lighten up, Kat, it's Hump Day!" Tyler, who isn't facing a deadline and certainly isn't worried about proving himself in this industry, calls back. "If you want, I can change it. Maybe some Rihanna on repeat? Work, work, work!"

I give him a glare that says I'm ready to work, not joke around. "As soon as the ode to Wednesday ends, can you turn it down though? I gotta focus and get this done."

"Will do," Tyler says. "Hey, Kat?"

"Yeah?"

"Kick some ass Friday. You know . . . because you're awesome."

I smile, feeling good that the guys around here support me. "Thanks, Tyler."

I sit down, reviewing the results of my last bug check. With a hundred thousand lines of code, it's a bitch to wrap my head around. Until now, it's been a matter of sending the app to various beta testers who put it through its paces, and then tracking down the errors they find.

But no amount of beta testing is going to be able to catch everything, so I hunker down, obsessively looking at my notes and trying to hunt down which lines need to be adjusted. It's hard, stressful work, and I'm running out of time.

Part of me knows I shouldn't stress. Lots of programs are released without being perfect. That's what updates and patches are for. But I really want to make sure this is good right off the bat so it doesn't get a bad rap.

Still, it's slow, dull work, and my mind keeps going to thoughts of Derrick. Since my talk with Elise where I realized how hard I was falling, and our subsequent confessions of 'I love you', we've texted constantly, even as he's given me time to do work. Pic exchanges helped some, but damn, there's no substitute for being in his arms.

The day wears on, lunch scarfed while I try to focus, but

by the time six o'clock rolls around, my eyes are half-crossed and I'm needing a break. Firing up my browser, I go to the website that lets me listen in to Derrick, ready for my own Love Whispering on my headphones.

"Good evening, it's my personal second favorite day of the week, Hump Day Wednesday," Derrick says, making me grin. At least someone enjoys Wednesdays, even if it's just for a corny opening joke.

"What's your favorite day of the week?" Susannah asks. "Friday?"

"Nope," Derrick replies. "Saturday. Get to sleep in, watch cartoons in my PJs, and have the whole day and night to do whatever, or whomever, I want."

You mean you have all evening to spend with me, if the last month or so has been any indication, I think. *I like Saturdays too.*

Susannah gives a grade-school-worthy "Ooh!" and her delight at Derrick's joke is palpable.

"Tonight's show is about something that could even be more important than actual bedroom performance," Derrick says.

"Wait, there's something more important?"

"Yep. What's the point of having all the best tricks in the toolbox if you never get a chance to show them off?" Derrick asks. "What I mean, of course, is flirting and the art of meeting someone. Now, unless you get all your dates off Craigslist, you gotta actually talk to someone and meet them. That takes guts and sometimes reading signals. Not everyone has a blinking sign on their chest that says 'take me to bed, you big stud.'"

"You and I must go to very different parties then," Susannah quips. "Personally, I just have to say one word . . . yes."

I giggle. Susannah's funny sometimes. Normally, she's not, but recently, she's been a lot more playful as Derrick's been more straight-talking, less flirty.

"Maybe that works for you," Derrick says, chuckling, "but for a lot of us, we need some help. I sure did."

"You?" I ask in stereo with Susannah. "How?"

"Way back when, I developed a crush on one of the girls in my school. She was pretty, a social leader, played on the girls' volleyball team, all that. I was a sophomore and basically ate, slept, and breathed football. Didn't have much practice talking to the opposite sex. Needless to say, she left me tongue-tied."

"Oh, really? Mr. Love Whisperer didn't know what to say?"

"Nope. Every time I had a chance to talk to her, I found myself acting stupid or posing awkwardly like I was Mr. Chill. In the end, I lost my chance. She started dating a guy, and they stayed together until they both graduated. That's okay. I've moved on and things are great, but lesson learned. Take the shot! I never even knew if she liked me back because I didn't know how to read her signs or if I was giving out any signs myself other than a Wyle E.

Coyote 'Help!' sign. Anyway, let's get to some callers. Who's up first, Suz?"

"First up, we've got Rich."

"How're you doing, Rich?"

The voice that comes on has to be partly played up. This guy sounds like he just came out of a *Dukes of Hazzard* re-run. *"Well D, I done got me an issue. You see, there's this lady that I see quite often. Actually, she's my hair stylist."*

"So you see her how often?" Derrick asks, and I lean forward, forgetting my work.

"About twice a month, but every time, I swear she's lookin' at me like she's interested. I mean, I know she's single, a little older than me but not too much, and she's as purty as they come. But I don't want to make it awkward if I approach her and she says no, know what I mean? I mean, I've got one of those heads of hair that just needs a good touch, and she's about the only one who can keep me from just saying fuck it and shaving the whole thing off."

The call continues, with Susannah taking most of the lead on that one. "A lot of how women flirt can be almost subtle, and it's a combination of things," she says. "For example . . . Derrick, describe what I'm doing."

"You just tossed your hair over your shoulder," Derrick says, and inside, I feel a little jealous.

"And now?"

"You did the same thing."

"Right, but this time, I smiled and kept eye contact for

longer. You see, when a woman is interested in a man, we usually play it like . . . well, Rich, do you fish?"

"Who doesn't like to fish?"

"That's up for another debate," Derrick says. "But go ahead, Suz."

"Sometimes, we try to play it like a fisherman trying to get that big bass to latch onto the hook. If we just throw ourselves out there, the fish knows either the bait's bad or it's just a trap to get them on a big fucking hook, right? But if you play it too hard, the fish will lose interest and move on to something easier. So sometimes, teasing a man along to see if they're really interested is the best way. But Rich, you'll never know if you don't try."

"And if there's a big fucking hook in the middle of the bait?"

"Some people call that marriage," Derrick jokes, and even I have to laugh at that one. "Seriously, though, sounds like good advice. If you think she's interested, and you're obviously interested, go for it. Not saying you have to show up next time singing Alan Jackson for her, but hell, man, call her up and ask if she wants to get a cup of coffee or go to dinner. Worst thing that could happen is she says no. Best thing . . . well, there's a lot of great things that can happen too. Even with big hooks."

The calls continue, and as I listen, I notice a trend. I realize the show is about flirting and how to ask the opposite sex out, but I can't shake the idea of Susannah flirting with Derrick, even if it's for the radio. Normally, I'm not the jealous, possessive type, but damn . . . I'm ready to kick some ass when the song break comes on and I fire off a text to Derrick.

How's the show coming along?

Fun, but I can't wait until it's over. Getting awkward.

Relief. He's upfront about what's happening, which means he's just doing this professionally. I can deal with that.

Me2. OK, gonna try and work. Call U after show.

Reassured a little, I turn back to my code as the show comes back on. "Okay, everyone, after spending the last hour or so talking about how ladies show attraction, let's talk about how men do it."

"Besides popping a stiffy, you mean."

"Obviously," Derrick says.

"Well, if that's the case, since I did you, you have to do me now," Susannah says. "I mean . . . well, that certainly didn't come out how I meant it."

I can hear bullshit in someone's voice . . . and I'd say right now, Derrick's studio stinks like a dairy farm.

Derrick laughs a little awkwardly. "You know, Suz, I think a list might be better, since our fans listen and don't watch. Quit pouting, Suz, we've only got a three-hour show."

Pouting? What the fuck, Derrick, are you blind? She's flirting with you right now! All that shit she's been doing for the past hour hasn't been for the show!

Derrick is trying to get back on topic while Susannah

tries to play it off. Finally, he gets around to listing how guys like to flirt. There's nothing all that groundbreaking from my point of view. Eye contact, compliments, smiles, brushing hair behind her ear, touching the small of her back.

Actually, listening to him makes me smile and forget the anger at Susannah. Derrick's done all those things to me, plus some. I blush, knowing that Derrick's little flirts fill my belly with warmth, and that he still does them makes me feel . . . I dunno, safe? Appreciated?

"Okay, time for another caller," Derrick says. "Now, we've been covering a lot of classical flirting, but our next caller's got a slightly more twenty-first-century problem. We've got Kim. Go ahead, Kim."

"Hi, Derrick," a slightly nervous girl says. *"I've been talking to this guy online. How do I know if he's flirting with me? A lot of guys just send me pickup lines, or after the bare minimum of back and forth conversation, they send dick pics. But what about the ones that aren't perverts?"*

Derrick hums. "Sounds like you've learned to avoid the sketchy ones. That's fishing . . . just looking for a hole to put a hook in. Some are just looking for some attention, maybe seeing if they can get some nudie pics without having to actually work for it. Now, maybe you want that —nothing wrong with casual hookups if that's what you both want. But if you want more, it's hard to get to really know someone through words on a tiny screen. Eventually, you need to talk and spend some time together. You need those physical clues."

Susannah speaks up in agreement. "You gotta look into their eyes for real. And be on the lookout everywhere. You might find the one person you've been looking for somewhere you go all the time, like the coffee shop, the gym, or work. Be open and friendly with everyone, and see who's receptive and then flirt away."

"That's kinda hard. I don't really have a lot of guys around."

Derrick chuckles. "Kim, roughly half of the population is male. They're around. I promise. Just stay open to finding them."

He ends the call and hums into the mic. "One other area of flirting we haven't addressed yet is the flirting you do after you've already snagged someone." His usual velvet radio voice has a hint of gravel, and I know it's for me, a signal that he's thinking of me with this topic. Warmth builds in my tummy.

"Even after you're in a relationship, flirting is still important. Send good morning and goodnight texts or calls. Get them little presents if something reminded you of them. It doesn't have to be anything big, just a sign you thought of them and what they'd like. Maybe get him a coffee cup from his favorite team to keep at your place, or buy her favorite lotion to keep at yours. Speak to each other, and more importantly, listen. Compliment them, their body, their brain, their talents. Your partner should always know what attracted you to them in the first place and what attracts you to them today, whether it's the same things or new things."

I smile, thinking that this is nearly a blueprint of how we

get along. He's right. Every day, he does something to remind me how I make him feel, and he helps me feel beautiful every day. He helps me feel like maybe, just maybe, there's a silver lining to the clouds in life. Maybe my little Styrofoam cup isn't so small after all and I can have a bigger slice of 'happily ever after' like the one Jessie has and the one my mom is finally getting.

It also reminds me that he needs to get that too. Reaching for my phone, I send him another text. *Just to let you know . . . you're the sexiest, kindest man I've ever met. Just thinking of you. Call me later.*

Count on it.

They take two more calls, nothing major, although one is cute as he says this is his chance to tell the girl he's interested in, and then they go to another song break, old-school Sophie B. Hawkins with *Damn, Wish I Was Your Lover.*

I jam out for a bit. This was a song Mom loved to sing along to before Carpool Karaoke was around, but after a moment, my phone rings. Derrick.

"I've only got a minute while the song plays," he says, his voice low, "but I was missing you. And thanks for the text."

"I miss you too, not just sex but actually being with you. In your arms, hearing your voice turn to gravel just for me. Just hanging out and spending time together."

Derrick growls lightly, and I know exactly how he feels. "Damn, Kitty Kat. I know you're busy and I don't want to take away from your work, but I need to be with you tonight. I need to touch you, feel you."

Just his words already have me simmering and I need him just as much. "How soon can you get home after work?"

"As soon as this song ends, we're wrapping up for the night," Derrick says. "Leave the office. I'll be home in less than an hour. Hey, Kat . . . wear that teddy and boy short set from the other night. I believe I promised to take them off with my teeth."

I whimper at the thought and remind myself that I need to start packing a backpack for nights like this. "Fuck, Derrick. Yes, you did. I'm gonna hold you to that promise. Oh, one other thing."

"What's that?"

"I'm dropping off my toothbrush too."

"Damn right, you are."

CHAPTER 19

DERRICK

*J*t's only thirty minutes later that I'm opening my front door, rushing to pick up my coffee cup from the table. Usually, there's a post-show meeting, but I bailed tonight with an excuse about having plans.

Susannah gave me the stink eye, but that seems to be her status quo lately. And it wasn't a lie, I do have plans. Specifically, to slip that sexy lace right off Kat's body, slow and easy with my teeth, licking all along her skin as I do so.

I rush to the bathroom and give my teeth a quick brush. Making love after spicy enchiladas for dinner is *not* a good idea, and I just get my mouth rinsed when there's a knock on the door, and I grin, looking at myself in the mirror. The man who looks back is overjoyed, not just horny, and I know I've found a woman who could really be for me like Mom was for Dad.

Opening the front door, my stomach leaps as I see Kat

standing there. There's none of the elevated heels, none of the little pretentious pieces of armor she used at first to hide her worry and insecurity. Instead, there's just a five-foot-two-inch, honey blonde beautiful woman in sweatpants and a zipped-up jacket, her eyes sparkling as she looks up at me. "Well, hello there, lover. Wondered if you might have space to put me up for the night?"

"I can think of a space I can fill," I joke, tugging her inside. She's got a backpack over her shoulder. She did just like I asked and brought clothes for tomorrow too, it looks like. "God, I missed you."

"I can tell," Kat says, setting her bag down and half jumping into my arms. "I missed you too. How was work?"

"Susannah's being kind of a tyrant, but I get it. I'm not exactly putting a hundred and ten percent into each show recently," I admit, hugging her tightly and nuzzling her neck. "I need a bit more practice at work-life balance, because I've found someone more important than my work."

"Mmm . . .anyone I know?" she teases, her eyes glinting with delight.

I look up at her, deviling her back. "Oh, just my new pet . . . Kitty Kat." I move back to her neck, nibbling at the soft skin, hoping I leave tiny marks to show she's mine.

Kat purrs. "God, that feels good. Really, Derrick. You make me feel special, worthy." Her words light me up, knowing that she's finally letting go of the chinks her life has left in her armor. She's developed her own self-confidence. She's always been worth so much more than she's received. I didn't change that. I just offered her what I could . . . all of me, and I'm proud that she's giving herself back to me. I trace along her jawline with my tongue, finding her lips in a breathy kiss. Our kiss deepens as I carry her through my living room, but she pulls back, her eyes alight with naughty heat. "Not the bedroom . . . not yet. I want you to have dessert first. Take me to the kitchen."

I nod, my brain swirling with excitement and anticipation for what Kat might have in her mind. Along with her blooming self-confidence, she's definitely unleashed her inner sex kitten. She said she was quiet, even repressed, but as we've explored together, she's relaxed and has shown that she has a deep well of passion inside her that I feel damn lucky to swim in.

I set her on the countertop and step back, watching as Kat unslings her backpack and opens it. The first thing she pulls out is a set of black heels, which she sets aside. "Tomorrow's work outfit. The rest is downstairs in the car."

"You have something for dessert in there for me?" I ask, and she nods, pulling out a jar of maraschino cherries. "Cherries?"

"Uh-huh," Kat says, unzipping her jacket. Underneath, she's only wearing the same see-through teddy she wore for our hot phone chat the other night. I can see her pink nipples already pulled tight, poking out the thin, silky fabric, inviting me to taste. "Just have to choose the right bowl." She opens the jar, plucking a single cherry out and holding it up, her tongue peeking out to swipe the small drop of juice off the fruit. "Here? Here . . .?" She asks as she traces the sweet fruit along her cleavage before pulling down her sweatpants to reveal panties that match her top. "Or maybe here?" She dangles the cherry right over her bare mound, visible through the sheer fabric.

Kat spreads her legs, and I can't help but lick my lips at the almost see-through window of her panties and I watch her puffy lips spread slightly. "I'm feeling a little gluttonous—might want more than one cherry," I tease, pulling my shirt off and stepping between her creamy thighs to snap my teeth around the cherry, pulling it roughly off the stem before swallowing it almost whole. I kiss her, the sweet tang of the cherries blending with our breaths as she sets the jar down on the counter to tangle her hands in the belt loops of my jeans, pulling me close as she wraps her feet around my legs, locking me in place as if there's anywhere else I'd rather be.

The cherries momentarily forgotten, like promised, I take the strap of her teddy in my teeth and slide it off, kissing down the exposed swell of her breast until I find the stiff, crinkled tip of her nipple. I run my tongue around the edge and then bite it gently, pulling her into my mouth and stretching her breast until she gasps. "Oh, fuck, Derrick . . . God, you're making my pussy so wet."

"Let's find out," I growl, reaching down and slipping my fingers inside her panties. She's more than wet. She's nearly dripping, and I let my fingers slide through her slick folds, teasing her lips and clit as I look in her eyes. "Who does this belong to?"

"You. Only you," Kat mewls, wiggling her hips as my thumb rubs over her clit. "I can't imagine anyone but you."

"Good, because all I am, all I have, belongs to you too," I promise. I dip two fingers deep inside her, brushing along her velvet walls as she squeezes me tightly. Pulling out my coated fingers, I smear her wetness over her other nipple before pulling back to lock my eyes on her perfect tits. "And sometimes, it's fun to mix your desserts."

I devour her coated breast, sucking and feasting upon her warm, sweet flesh until I can't wait any longer. I kiss my way down her body, tracing designs with my tongue around her belly button and making her giggle. "I thought you were going to make me come, not laugh."

"Why not both?" I reply, grinning up at her. I see the jar of cherries and reach over as I lay her back, her petite frame and wide hips perfect for keeping her balance on the countertop. Uncapping the cherries, I peel her panties off before letting a drizzle of the bright red syrup flow over her glistening lips. Kat watches, her breasts heaving as she breathes deeply in anticipation. "Mmm, looks tasty."

"I hope I can have a big banana split later," Kat teases, licking her lips. I nod and kiss up the inside of her thigh, letting my warm breath play over her wet folds until she's squirming in need.

"Be still or you'll spill it all. Tell me, Kat. Tell me what you need." I can feel the tension in her thighs as she tries to fight the urge to lift her hips toward my mouth.

"Oh, Derrick . . . don't tease me. Lick my pussy. Taste me. Please."

"I can never deny you, especially when that's exactly what I want too," I growl, looking up her body into her beautiful eyes. Keeping my eyes locked on her, I drag my tongue through the sweet juice and syrup-covered folds of her pussy, tasting every nerve ending crackling along my tongue as Kat shivers, moaning from deep in her chest.

"Yes . . . that's it, make me come," Kat says, grinding her pussy against my lips. I dive in, taking turns using my tongue to lick up and down her silky lips and nibbling on her soft flesh, the sweet sugar of the cherries mixing with Kat's natural taste and making my head whirl. I cup her ass, pulling her close as I feast on her.

Kat's naturally spicy and tangy and sweet. Irresistible, and I know that half of my daydreams of Kat are filled with memories of how she tastes.

I nip lightly at her inner thigh and she bucks, begging, "Derrick . . .more." I understand. She needs something intense, something that will ground her and let her soar. I could happily lick and suck her for hours, but after all the teasing we've given each other tonight, she needs something now. I bite each inner thigh harder as I thumb her clit, leaving a round imprint of my teeth, praying that the outline stays. Some dark place inside me likes that she'll have that reminder of my claim on her.

Satisfied with the visual, I nibble at her clit, biting, not hard, but just enough to set her body shaking, her ass rising off the countertop as she cries out, coming hard. I keep sucking and biting her clit as she pulses, loving every quiver of her body as she unleashes on me.

When she sags to the countertop, I pull back, standing up to gather her in my arms. "You're fucking delicious. I want your taste on my tongue all the fucking time."

"Your turn," Kat says, wiggling. "You can fuck me later . . . but I've got a few tips from the Love Whisperer I've been wanting to try."

I set Kat down, and she gets on her knees, reaching for the waistband of my jeans. She doesn't have to do much. I'm so fucking hard by everything I've just done that my cock nearly bursts my zipper, and Kat chuckles, watching it bob in time with my racing heartbeat. "You look like you're about three seconds from coming down my throat."

"You know I'm better than that," I boast, but she's pretty much right. Still, I spread my legs a little, watching as Kat reaches up, fondling my balls in her soft hands before rolling them gently, tugging them down and relieving a little bit of the pressure that's building inside me. I moan, reaching down to stroke a hand through her hair as she reaches up with her other hand, barely wrapping her fingers around the base of my cock as she brings her face closer, rubbing the head with her cheeks, moaning and closing her eyes. "Fuck me, Kitty Kat. You're good."

"One of the lessons that I've been taught," she says, her eyes gleaming as she gives me feather-light butterfly kisses up and down my shaft. I moan. She's amazing. "And I can see you love it."

"I love everything you do," I tell her, groaning as she licks my cock from base to tip before spreading her lips and sucking just the head of my cock like a lollipop. "But damn, you have talent."

I can't form any more words as Kat continues. From running her tongue just around the head and then down the bottom and around the spot that she knows makes my toes curl, she uses every hint that I've ever talked about on my show to tease out my pleasure. I'm brought to new heights, my cock throbbing nearly painfully as my brain swims in pulses of light. I can't stand the teasing anymore, my voice gone as I growl. "Suck me, Kat. Suck that cock down like my good girl." Kat slowly bobs up and down on my cock, her cheeks hollow as she swallows my entire shaft before pulling back.

I wish it could go on forever, this feeling that she's creating in me. Never before have I felt so powerful, this honey-blonde angel lovingly worshipping my cock. Kat closes her eyes, pinching her nipples with her right hand before slipping it between her legs, rubbing her pussy in time with her head. "That's it," I rasp, watching her fingers speed up. "Touch yourself for me. Rub your needy little clit so you come when I do. Swallow me all down, baby."

Kat mumbles something that sounds like 'yes' around my cock and sucks faster, her tongue caressing and stroking every inch of my shaft. She reaches up, grabbing my left hand and guiding it to the back of her head. Gathering her hair in my fist, I use it to hold her still as I start pumping my cock in and out of her eager mouth. Her moans increase in pitch and volume until we're both groaning and gasping while Kat takes me all the way, burying the head of my cock in her throat and swallowing. "Oh shit, babe . . . is this what you want? You want me to fuck your face like you're my dirty little slut? God damn, you are so fucking sexy. I'm gonna come, Kat. You ready?"

I pull back just as Kat starts shaking, her fingers pumping in and out of her pussy so fast that her hips jerk, and we both go over the edge. I cry out, my cock filling her mouth with my cream as Kat's groans vibrate to the very depths of my soul. I think I say her name, but if I do it's so swallowed up in the heat of my orgasm that all that comes out is something primal, animal.

This is the woman I love. This is the woman I need for as long as I live. "Holy shit, babe . . . you didn't miss a single bit."

"Good," Kat says, getting up and kissing me softly. "Now, how about some real dessert to get our strength up, and then you can have one last round before we hit the bed? And this one, cowboy, is going to be very special."

"Why's that?" I ask, kissing the tip of her nose. I've gotta have some ice cream or something around here some-where. I eat right, but not perfectly.

"Because if you want, how about you do a little research and practice for that anal episode you're going to do?" she asks. "I figure I'm ready. If you want to."

I look into her eyes and see the mix of desire, excitement, love, and yes, a big helping of fear in there, and it fills my heart with an intense need to do this right. "Of course. On one condition. You say stop, I stop. No judgement, no worries. Agreed?"

Kat's eyes sparkle in tears and she kisses my chest. "Agreed." Her voice tickles across me as she lays her cheek against my chest, wrapping her arms around my waist. "Derrick, I'm . . . a little scared."

I lean down to kiss the top of her head, hugging her back. "Hey, no pressure. We don't have to do anything you don't want to."

I feel her smile against me, "Not about that—well, not really. Just this, *us*. I've really never felt like this before, and it's scary. It feels big, and you've got me dreaming of things I never thought I'd be dreaming about. Like a future. Like forever."

I take a big breath, knowing that this is a turning point for her and for us. We've said 'I love you' and meant it and have woven ourselves together into a routine that's become the focal point of my life, and those things are easy for me, both because of who I am and more importantly, who *she* is. But it's more difficult for her to trust, to believe and hope. I want to be worthy of her heart, even if I have to earn it every day for the rest of our lives. "Kat, I've got you and I won't hurt you. I love you."

She leans back, looking up at me. "Thank you. For everything." And with a bearhug-tight squeeze, she shifts the mood. "All right, let's get some damn cookies!"

CHAPTER 20

*T*he faces around the table look slightly less than convinced, and there's a little bit of sweat trickling down the small of my back as the twin projectors pump heat through the room.

"So how is this supposed to be targeted to the female audience?" one of them asks. "There's not a lot of real on-the-surface differences between your app and the competitors already on the market."

"On the surface, you're right," I reply. "It's when you get into the guts and the way the app seamlessly and uniquely integrates various systems within the architecture of the pre-existing operating system and apps that makes it a winner."

"But what's the marketing angle? Your user interface is rather plain. Nothing really screams feminine."

I squirm, feeling the heat. They're really coming at me.

"If by feminine you mean frilly laces and a lot of pink fonts and motifs, you're right, this isn't feminine," I reply. "This is meant for the modern powerful female, the post-*#MeToo*er who's kicking ass and taking names at work and in her personal life. Because she's making a name for herself in the office, she's gotta look professional. So the interface does look professional . . . except that it's going to have that perspective that's going to give her the edge she needs in her life."

"So twenty-first-century Boss Bitch?" someone else, part of the marketing group, asks. "I like the sound of it and I think I can work with that. How's the guts of it?"

"As good as any other app in the category, and better in a lot of ways," I say. "It's lean. There's no bloat, so it runs faster. Let me give you a test drive."

The meeting continues, and while there are a few times I have to really drive my point home hard, I feel like it went easier than my last app presentation. Maybe it's that I've earned at least a little cred with these people . . . but more than anything, I think it's the newfound strength and confidence I've had since meeting Derrick. I've always felt pretty confident in myself when it came to work, but I can't help but feel that his giving me more personal confidence has given me that extra leg up when talking to these guys. It's not only that Derrick makes me feel sexy. I just feel like I'm starting to truly understand the strength and power that come from my own femininity, and that's a huge plus considering I create apps for the modern female demographic.

"You know, Katrina," one of the company vice-presidents

says after playing with the app for almost an hour, "this app of yours, while I guess it's got a feminine touch, is just a good app for everyone. Can we consider just marketing it to the general public or giving it a slightly different skin and releasing it again as a partner app for men?"

"We will whip up presentations for both ideas," the marketing guru says. "Either way, with the muscle behind this hustle . . . congrats, Kat. I think you've got your next number one on your hands."

The congratulations go around the table, and I feel like I'm floating, damn-near seven feet tall as I walk out. Reaching my cubicle, I flop down, kicking off my high heels and rubbing my toes. Another sign that I'm getting comfortable with myself is that these stripper heels aren't daily wear anymore. I still like wearing something that elevates me, but only because it makes it easier to kiss Derrick.

"Tomorrow, I'm wearing stacked heel boots," I promise myself as I pull out my phone. I hit the speed dial, knowing I might not reach him but I promised him I'd give him a call as soon as my meeting was over.

Before the call can connect, one of the company Vice Presidents, a forty-three-year-old tech geek named Edgar, knocks on the edge of my wall. "Katrina?"

"Hi, Edgar," I reply, setting my phone down. "How can I help you?"

"I think you can help the company in a lot of ways, actually," he says. "Because your app is streamlined and clean.

What would you think about being a team leader for the new game app we're developing?"

"Team leader? Game app?" I ask, surprised. "I'd love the opportunity, but are you sure? Games haven't really been my experience, and most of those guys have been at it for a long time."

"That's exactly why you're the man—woman—for the job. Bring in some new blood, different perspective than what they're used to. Maybe find a way to bring the conciseness of your coding style to the game side because they're always working to balance the functionality with the size and speed of the game. You've proven yourself, and I'm confident you'll whip them into shape."

"I . . . of course! Can we discuss the details Monday?"

Edgar nods, flashing me a grin. "Enjoy your successful presentation. We'll talk about the future Monday morning."

He leaves, and I blink before a small sound from my desk makes me realize . . . "Derrick?"

"Hey, Kitty Kat, I got to hear the good news," Derrick says in my ear. "Always knew you were as smart as you are beautiful." He's switched to his deeper, richer voice and it fills me with heat.

"Yeah, well, right now, I'm wearing lined granny panties and squirming in my chair because of you," I tease back. "Thanks."

"Anytime, love. So, you nailed me . . . I mean, you nailed

the presentation, I take it?" Derrick asks, making me chuckle.

"Honey, as good as I feel right now, I'm feeling like a million bucks," I purr, dropping my voice. "I've got the sexiest man in the world, and I feel like I can do any damn thing I want."

"That's because you can," Derrick says. "Listen, can we get together tonight then? My place, your place, I don't care. I just want one of us to come to the other, then we'll both come together. Guaranteed."

I shake my head and look up to wave off another congrats from one of the other coders in the cubicle crew. "Sorry, babe. I was already told before the meeting that the whole Geek Patrol is going out to celebrate, and it'll be late. I think someone's already got their Jedi robes ready."

"Jedi robes?" Derrick asks, and I laugh.

"I'm just kidding. We're not that far gone. How about tomorrow afternoon, I come over to your place and we spend the whole rest of the weekend together?"

I can hear his smile even through the phone, and the naughty lilt to his voice. "Twenty-four-hour wait . . . by then, I'm going to be ready to pound you into total submission, my little Kitty Kat. I've got a confession. You've got me addicted to your sweet taste, your tight pussy. I need you every day, at least once a day."

"Don't worry, you've got me the same way. If I'm not getting a big, throbbing Vitamin D injection at least daily,

I feel empty . . . speaking of which, I'm feeling a little empty now."

"Oh, don't tease me," Derrick growls. "I'm already keeping Susannah waiting for our pre-show meeting . . . and I want to give you the time you deserve. And let's be honest, you're not in a place to turn on your video either."

"Nah," I admit. "The cubicle's a little . . . lacking in sound-proofing. But later, maybe I can find some privacy to show you something."

"Mmm . . . you know you always knock my socks off," Derrick replies. "Listen, babe, I'm thinking, if you want to stay the weekend, bring some more stuff over. You know, just in case you want to stay longer or something."

I smile. "Careful there, love. You're going to regret it when I bring in a hundred pairs of shoes and take over your closet."

"You don't have a hundred pairs of shoes."

I laugh, mockingly evil. "Bwahaha, after this app hits number one and I get gamer coding bankroll, I might go shoe shopping!"

Derrick laughs. "Add in a couple more pairs of fuck-me pumps, and I'm happy. You can wear them while I make you scream my name in ecstasy."

"You mean like this?" I ask, lowering my voice to my breathiest whisper. "Oh, Derrick . . . yes, baby, please. God, I need you to fuck me."

The answering moan on the other end of the line is all I need, and I smile. "I love you."

"I love you too, Kat." There's a holler on the other end of the line, and Derrick growls. "I'll be there in a minute!"

He comes back on, slightly abashed. "Okay, babe, if I don't go now, Susannah's going to be doing a special show tonight on castration with a pair of office scissors."

"Can't lose those. I need them too much." I laugh. "Go do your meeting. I love you."

"I love you too. Bye. And congrats."

The line goes dead, and I lean back, smiling to myself. A great presentation, a huge opportunity, and I think a backdoor invitation to move in if I want with the man of my dreams?

How'd this happen? For so long, I thought this sort of life wasn't possible. That I'd never have a chance to have it all, a good man, a good job, and best of all, some actual inner peace. I thought I'd always be hustling, worried about what others would say about me, that I'd never be able to get on top . . . and suddenly, I feel like I am. And the view up here is fucking awesome.

The old me would be looking for the other shoe to drop any time now, but that was the old me. The new me, she's going to celebrate with her co-workers. And tomorrow, I'm going lingerie shopping before going over to Derrick's so we can do our own kind of celebrating.

"Like the man said, it don't get much better than this."

CHAPTER 21

DERRICK

"*S*o anyway, we're going to spend the last hour doing an interview with a woman who's making a series of videos . . ."

I let Susannah's words just descend into a sort of buzz in the background. Hell, I can't even pretend to focus on what she's saying in the pre-show meeting because my head is in the clouds with thoughts of Kat and how well she's doing.

Hey, babe, I read, looking down at my phone, *just leaving work now. Wish you were here, but I'll try and catch your show later. Love you.*

I smile, earning a growl from Susannah. "For fuck's sake, Derrick, you said you were done with that."

"I'm listening. You know I'm always impromptu," I lamely defend myself. "I got it. Guest coming in, makes videos, blah, blah."

"That blah, blah is what's going to make up the last hour of the show," she shoots back. "Or do you plan on pissing this one off like you did the last?"

"Hey, I can't help we didn't agree," I reply. Before I can continue, my phone buzzes again. I don't even have a chance to look down before Susannah erupts.

"Dammit, Derrick, it won't hurt you to turn that thing off for a while! You didn't even hear what I said about her, did you?

I feel a bit bad. She's right in that I have no idea what the hell this guest is about, but hoping to salve her temper tantrum, I set my phone aside and focus my full attention on her. "Let's start over. What's this guest's deal?"

Susannah shakes her head, tossing her clipboard aside. Rubbing at her temples, she looks up, taking a big breath before answering. "You've been completely off your game for over a month now. After I found out why, I've cut you some slack. But things haven't gotten better. If anything, they've gotten worse. You're distracted during the shows, barely talking to me before or after, and just generally being an asshole. We've got a good thing here, I think, and you're ruining it for some chick of the week. You need to ditch the needy bitch."

I slam my hand down on the table, pissed off. "She's not a chick of the week, and don't you dare call her a bitch. What the fuck, Susannah? You know I don't fuck around like that. Kat and I have something serious going on here. I'm sorry if I've been distracted during the show, but we're doing fine other than your trying to dictate my every word and action. You're not my boss, Susannah. We have a good thing going with the show, but let's keep it there. Stay out of my personal life."

"That's it?" Susannah shoots back. "That's it, like all we've done is do shows about gardening or some lame ass Top 40 countdown. In case you haven't noticed, I know more about your sex life than even your avid listeners do. Hell, I've been able to see when you're talking book talk, and when you're talking fantasies, and when you're talking real-life experiences. You've seen the same from me."

"We work together. That's the nature of the show. Of course you know a lot about me. I don't get what your point is. "

"I'm just fucking pissed, Derrick. I've poured my guts into this show and I thought you were too. It works because we bounce off each other and balance each other's style. Now you're just phoning it in? That's bullshit and it's only a matter of time before it costs us."

Her little speech puts me on my heels, and I look down, wondering if she's right. I've checked our ratings. They're still holding strong, even if Susannah is freaking out. "Suz, I've never been a prepper. The show's doing okay, and we're fine on-air. I'm sorry if you feel like I'm not giving you as much focus, but I'm as committed as I've always been. You need to chill out."

Susannah sighs. "I wasn't going to say anything until we got something harder on the plate, but there's been a few feelers by a production company. They're talking national syndication plus maybe TV or Internet video broad-casting our shows too."

"What?" I ask, shocked. I've heard nothing about this. "Why haven't I been told?"

"Well, you *would* have, but you haven't stuck around. It'd be a lot like how Stern and some of the other talk radio people have their shows broadcast. They'll set up a couple of hard cameras in a new studio that they'll pay for, and then we do our show like normal. But none of that can happen unless these guys see you at the top of your game. I'm doing everything I can to hold this shit together and grow the show, but I can't do it by myself."

I blink, stunned. "Okay . . . okay, you've got a point. But Suz, and this is serious, if you're mad at me, leave it work-related. It's not Kat's fault, so leave her out of it. I think I may have found *the one*, and I'm not going to listen to that."

I see something glimmer in Susannah's eyes, but she nods. "Okay then, agreed. Now, about tonight's show."

"Yeah," I say, putting aside the bad feelings. We aired them out and it's over. Kinda like when I was in football and two guys on the team had beef. We'd hash it out, some-times a punch or two was thrown, but after that, it was time to play the game and turn that anger against our opponents. "I get the feeling there's something unique about her. You said videos. What's the deal?"

Before Susannah can speak, my phone rings again. "For fuck's sake!"

"Sorry," I reply, looking down.

She's right back pissed again, muttering under her breath. "Of course you're going to answer it, regardless of what you just said. Her little lap dog, running whenever she calls or texts a damn thing." She stomps out of the room, venomous contempt dripping from every word.

Knowing we'll definitely have to revisit that since apparently, our truce from mere moments ago didn't last, I growl and answer the call. "Dad?"

Dad's breathing is heavy and labored, and inside, I immediately start to worry. "Derrick, I'm so sorry."

"Dad, what's wrong?" I ask, standing up. "What's happening?"

"I was outside, moving stuff around in the shed, and . . ." he says, gasping for air and groaning. "My heart. I think I'm having a heart attack."

"Dad, I'm calling 9-1-1." I go to grab a desk phone, but he stops me.

"Already called. They're on their way. Derrick, I love you, son. I'm damn proud of you." There's a tone to his voice that sounds like he's trying to say goodbye.

Choking back a sob, I growl at the phone, "I know, Dad. I love you too, but don't do that. You're gonna be okay. I'm gonna meet you at the hospital."

I keep talking, but I'm running out of the office to my car. The show never even crosses my mind as I peel out of the lot and head toward the hospital.

"Dad, I met someone. She's the one and I'm going to marry her. I want you to meet her, so you gotta fight. Just like you always taught me when football got tough. You gotta keep fighting, okay?"

"Okay, son . . . they're here." There's a jostling sound on the phone and a woman's voice comes on the line.

"Hello? We're taking him to City Center Hospital. You can meet us there."

I think I say okay, but then it's just dead air. There's not much traffic, and I'm admittedly driving way too fast, but it still feels like forever and a day to get there.

Rushing inside, I get help from the first nurse I see. "I'm here to see Daniel King. He was just brought in. I'm his son."

She leads me over, but other than looking in through a glass window to see a man who has my father's face but I swear looks about twenty years older, there's nothing I can do. I pace back and forth in the hallway, doing my best not to get in the way as nurses and doctors come in and out. Occasionally, I hear some medical jargon that scares me, but before I can even ask them what the hell 'hs-CRP' or 'Troponins test' means, they're gone. I'm left to sit in a chair by the door, staring down at the tile and hoping that the next time a doctor comes out, it's not to tell me it's time to say goodbye to my father.

"Mr. King?"

I look up. It's nearly eight o'clock now, but the doctor

who's looking down at me has a relieved look on his face. "Is he . . .?"

"I think we've gotten him out of the woods," the doctor says as he holds out a hand. "Glen Stoker. I'm the on-call cardiologist. When your father was brought in, it was for a suspected myocardial infarction . . . a heart attack. We've confirmed that he did, in fact, have a pretty severe MI. We've stabilized him for now, and I think he's out of the woods. He looks like he's normally a pretty active guy, so that's in his favor."

"He is," I confirm, standing up to look at Dad. He's sleeping, but I can see the heart monitor next to his head, and the little wiggly line reassures me. "He's been on blood pressure and cholesterol meds for a few years, but nothing like this has ever happened."

"We'll have to keep him here a few more days and talk with his primary care doctor. Do you have that information?"

"I think he's still going to Dr. Jack Reynolds. I don't have his number though. That's at home."

"That's okay, I know Jack," Dr. Stoker says. "Listen, it'll be a few minutes before we can have a room ready for him. For now, though, he'd do better if his son was with him. And Mr. King?"

"Yeah?" I ask, not looking at the doctor at all.

"He's in good hands here. For now, just make sure he stays calm."

I go inside the exam room, where the beeping of the

various machines still reassures me that my father is still alive. Looking down at him, he looks so old, so frail . . . my vision doubles, then blurs, and before I know, it tears are running down my face as I reach down, blindly taking his hand.

"I never told you how much you mean to me," I whisper, afraid to wake him. "But I promise you, you're going to find out. You think you never understood why I do what I do . . . but I'm just trying to tell the world that love, real love, like what you and Mom had . . . it does exist. And I want to do everything in my power to make sure that type of love doesn't die. I love you, Dad."

In the movies, he'd wake up right now, maybe whisper a few words, either sarcastic or loving, depending on the type of movie. But this isn't a movie. This is real life, and all I can do is sit down in another chair and rest my forehead against the bars on the side of his bed.

I want to call Kat. I need to hear her voice telling me it'll be okay, but in my haste of rushing into the hospital, I left my phone in the car and I can't leave right now.

It'll be all right, for now. She's out with friends, happy and celebrating. I don't want to ruin her celebration. I know how hard she worked for this. I'll let her enjoy the evening and when dad gets transferred up to his room, I'll slip out and grab my phone.

It'll be late, but I need to hear her voice.

CHAPTER 22

KAT

*T*he bar, one of those weird little spots that could only exist in a city near a university with a large computer science department and plenty of techies like me, is rockin' for the type of customers it collects. On one side of the place, three of the interns from the company are engaged in a sick *StarCraft* battle royale, while around my table are a gaggle of people tossing back European microbrews, trying to look hipster and utterly failing. But we're having a blast, and that's all that matters.

"So, what's next?" my co-worker asks as he looks over at me. "Plan to take over the world?"

I shake my head, sipping at my wine. "Nope, team lead for the new game app. Apparently, they need a healer."

It's a cheesy as fuck joke, but I've already downed a few glasses, and we're all at that point where we can set aside our worries and just be silly. Thankfully, everyone else is maybe drunker than I am, and they all laugh even if it wasn't that funny.

Cheers go up, each of them congratulating me. I finish off the glass of Merlot I'm drinking, and just as I set my glass down, my phone rings. I grin, figuring it's Derrick on a song break on his show.

I hate that I'm missing it tonight. Listening in has gotten to be such a daily dirty habit. His voice coming through my stereo, or even my earbuds, all sex and silk, just warms me up for when he whispers dirty things in my ear later, that softness turning to sex just for me. Sure, it's meant a few nights of working different hours . . . but then again, I'd say the benefits have been more than worth it.

I look at my phone and see that it's not Derrick.

It's Elise. Getting up, I head out into the chilly night air, where it's not quite so insane and the cool helps me clear my head. Still, the music is easily heard. "Hey Elise! What's up?"

"Kat? Where are you? It's loud on your end. Can you hear me?"

"Sorry, I'm out with people from work. They loved my new app. We're sort of celebrating. Why, what's up?"

"So you're not listening to the show right now?"

There's something in Elise's voice that does more than the cool air to pierce through my wine-induced haze. "No, why? Should I be?"

"Honey," Elise says in that voice that she uses whenever

shit's hit the fan somewhere and she knows I'm going to need her to be strong, "I need you to come to my place right now. Wherever you are, whatever you're doing, just stop and come here now."

The fact that Elise isn't telling me what's going on scares me, and I rub at my face, another part of me already in emergency procedure mode. I need to settle tonight's bar tab, get a ride, get to Elise, and . . . well, I don't know from there. Ugh, I hate being buzzed and adult at the same time. "Elise, what's wrong? What aren't you telling me?"

"Just come," Elise says. "Now. Get over here."

That settles it. I trust her with my life. "I'm on my way."

I head back into the bar, prepared to make half-hearted excuses, but as soon as he sees me, Tyler sets his drink aside. "You okay?"

"A friend called. Something important came up," I tell him. "Listen, can you cover the tab? I mean, I don't want to . . ." I look at the door, the urgency live in my chest.

"You can PayPal me the tab on Monday," Tyler says, waving me off before hooking a thumb at the assembled crew. "As long as these fuckers don't drink five thousand dollars of cheap beer and wine, I think we're okay."

"Deal. Thanks, Tyler."

I gather my purse and head out the door, flagging down the first taxi I see to head to Elise's place. "Hey," I ask as I settle in, "you got satellite radio?"

"Sure do, this baby's almost brand-new," the driver says. "Whatcha want me to put on?"

"Think you can put on The Love Whisperer?" I ask. "Channel fifty-seven I think."

"No problem," the cabbie says. He turns his dial a few times, and soon enough, *The Love Whisperer* pops up. "You ain't the first lady who's asked to listen to that guy. He's got a voice that could talk the panties off a mannequin."

They're in a song break, and when they come back, my heart skips a beat.

"We're back, everyone," Susannah says, and I give the radio a raised eyebrow. What the hell? *"I'm Susannah Jameson, and welcome back to The Love Whisperer. We're continuing our evening chat on technology in dating before getting to our special guest tonight. More specifically, how to use technology to spice up your love life and get you to the bedroom, since some folks need a little help even getting there for some real-time action."*

"Ain't that the damn truth," the cabbie mutters.

"So let's continue our discussion of phone sex and video chat sex and how it can spice things up for long-distance relationships and new hook-ups. Or even for regular Joes-and-Bettys who want to try something a little more . . . dirty, raunchy, or dare I say . . . naughty. Whether its Skype, FaceTime, or whatever new app you like, technology can lend a lot of fun to your nighttime activities. Hell, maybe your daytime ones too. But really, once you decide to try a little verbal foreplay beyond just flirting, what do you actually say? Any suggestions, oh Love Whisperer?"

There's a pause and Derrick's satin voice comes across the radio, *"Just keep it hot, hot, hot, and it'll do the trick. Guaranteed."*

There's a hint to Susannah's voice that I don't like, an edge that makes me think things aren't right with her. She sounds . . .angry. And I wonder what's happening in the studio to cause that. Maybe something happened on air? Did she and Derrick have an argument? Maybe that's what Elise is calling about?

"Now, we've played a few clips already, as shared by our generous Love Whisperer from his personal collection, but we saved this one for last, the crème de la crème of some crazy-hot phone sex. Make sure you've got a pen to take notes, listeners. Maybe a towel too . . . for the drool." She giggles throatily. *"Let's take a listen, and we'll open up the lines for you after this."*

Derrick chuckles, saying, *"Let's hear it."* And there's a split second before the recording starts.

From the first grunt, all the blood rushes from my face as I recognize who it is. *"You know I love your tits,"* Derrick growls. *"Show those perfect tits to me. Rub your thumb across your nipples until they're pearled up for me."*

It's edited, but not for content. Instead, every mention of emotion, every dimming of anything except lewd, nasty fucking sex is stripped out. I listen as my voice comes through the radio, mewling that yes, I'm Derrick's dirty little slut, my breath audibly quickening and the squelching noises obvious even over the radio as I finger fucked myself for him.

Just as I call out his name, the cabbie reaches over, switching it off. The taxi driver looks at me in the rearview mirror, "Sorry, Miss, that's a bit much for me. The wife would skin me alive for listening to something like that with a lady in the car."

I nod absently, the ice in my gut rushing through my entire body. Why is there a recording of our conversations? What's this shit about a personal collection?

I thought those were private, just Derrick and me. I guess he never said that, but obviously, I assumed. Why *wouldn't* they be? And why would he play them on the air?

Oh, God, I've been getting played this entire time. The thought hits me like a grenade in the stomach, and the shakes start. I'm barely keeping it together when the taxi pulls up to Elise's apartment and she's outside waiting for me.

"I can tell by the look on your face that you already know. What the fuck is happening, Kat?"

Her matter-of-fact tone gives me some stability, and I hug myself, shaking my head. "I don't know. That's us, our private conversations. Why?"

Elise gives the cab driver his fare and leads me into her place. "I don't know what's going on, but that shit's not okay."

"Why would he even record them in the first place?" I ask softly, hurt and confused. "I . . . they weren't meant for the public. They were me, baring my heart to him."

Elise looks at me with pity, then sighs. "Well, I could see

why he would. They're pretty fucking hot. Maybe he was just recording them for later . . . spank bank type deal?"

I snort. If Derrick needed spank bank material, all he had to do was give me a call, the way we've gotten it on over the past few weeks. "He never told me he was recording me . . . us. Oh, God, Elise! He played it on the air, and everyone heard me have an orgasm and tell how hungry for his cock I am. He said my name!"

The last fact saps the last of my reserve and I dissolve into tears. Elise does what she can as she gathers me up, pulling me into a hug. I collapse on the couch and she covers me with a blanket, mistaking my shivers of heartbreak as cold. "It'll be okay, Kat. I listened to the first couple before calling you. He said your name, but there's gotta be what, a million 'Kats'? Nobody can prove it was you."

She rushes into the kitchen, making me a cup of coffee, but I just hold it, not able to take a sip with my heart in my throat.

"People will know," I whisper. "God, he's been to my place. I've been to his. Kevin knows I've been with him . . . it'll get out, Elise. If Kevin knows, he'll make sure of it. It'll get out, and I'll be ruined."

Elise slips an arm around my shoulders, hugging me from the side. "You need to call him. Figure out what the hell is going on!"

I sigh, looking into the black mirror that is the surface of my coffee. "You're right. Maybe there's some reason . . ." I

LAUREN LANDISH

look up at Elise again, but the truth is clearly written on her face. "Guess not, huh?"

Elise shakes her head. "Damn it, Kat. I'm so sorry. I pushed you into this. I really thought he was a good guy with all the things you said about him."

"I felt like I had a good feel of him from our dates and his show too, but I guess that's all façade. Love Whisperer, my ass. God, I should've known better. Hell, I do know better! Guys are always out for themselves and a piece of ass. But he made me believe, and I played right into his hands. This hurts so much worse than before because he made me . . . hope." The tears come, hot and burning as they roll down my face, and I cry my heartbreak out for Elise, who strokes my hair and kisses my forehead.

"I promise you, Kat, I don't care if the whole gender of men is going to hell. I'm right here with you."

"I guess I need to get this over with," I whisper. I reach into my bag, grabbing my phone. It hurts to see his name in my recent contacts, surrounded with little heart-eyed face emojis, but I need to get this over with before I lose my nerve. And I need answers.

The call rings . . . and rings . . . and rings. "Hey, you've reached Derrick King. Leave me a message. Or, as this is the twenty-first century, send me a text. Bye."

The phone beeps, and I clear my throat before speaking, but my voice is still wavering. "Derrick, it's Kat. You need to call me."

As I hang up, I look at the time and I realize the show is

over. He should be able to pick up his phone if he wanted to, just like he has countless times before. He's avoiding my call. Ignoring me after what he's done. He doesn't have the balls to face me.

The ice in my veins freezes. He'd systematically broken down all my defenses from the beginning, one by one, pecking away at them to get me to open up to him, and he make me think he was one of the good guys. But he lied. This is so much worse than Kevin or my other boyfriends cheating on me. This is a public betrayal at a foundational level. I loved him, truly and deeply, and I thought he loved me. But obviously not if he can air our private life without even asking me. Fuck, he even joked and laughed about it, like it was no big deal.

I don't know why he'd do this, but fuck him if he thinks I'm some fuck toy he can screw around with.

I'm done with him, done with men.

Forever.

I turn my phone off and hug Elise as the tears roll down my face. I'll cry out every last tear so that there's nothing left and then I'll turn my heart off and never risk loving some backstabbing asshole again.

I'm done, my heart shattered into unfixable shards in my chest.

CHAPTER 23

DERRICK

*T*he sun is just creeping over the horizon when I can sneak out of the hospital and down to my car to grab my phone.

It was a long night. Once Dad was transferred, he'd woken up a little but was disoriented. I was uncomfortable leaving him alone, even with nurses twenty feet away and watching the monitors.

I stayed by his bedside until he fell into a fitful sleep. I drifted off soon after, uncomfortably perched in a chair beside him until the shift-change nurse woke us both to take his vitals.

Turning on my phone, I see it's been blowing up all night. I've got several missed calls from Jacob, one from Kat . . . but more worrisome, at least two dozen calls from Susannah and the station number.

I rub the back of my neck, not sure what I'm going to do. I knew I'd likely get shit for bailing on the show with no notice, but what the hell did they want me to do? My dad was having a heart attack.

If Susannah couldn't handle things, there are plenty of archived shows they could air if need be. We already do that on our two nights off each week, and listeners seem to like the classics. If Suz was in a lurch, she could've just punched play on one of those.

Yeah, shitty on my part to duck like I did, but a necessary deal when there's a medical emergency. I decide to give Jacob a call first. He doesn't call often so it must have been important for him to call multiple times. Kat was probably just checking in to tell me everything was going okay and she was being safe. I won't wake her up with the bad news just yet.

Besides, Jacob will want to know. He and Dad got pretty friendly back in my college days, and Jacob really took a liking to my father, often hanging out at the house when the lifestyle of being a superstar student-athlete with a professional future got to be a bit too much to deal with.

I hit *Dial* and lean against my car, yawning as the cold morning air wakes me up.

As soon as Jacob picks up the line, however, all sleepiness is driven from me when he yells, "What the fuck, man?!"

"Hey, bro, I know it's early as fuck. You just don't normally call multiple times like that. Besides, aren't you usually up at this hour?"

"What the hell are you doing? The show last night? How could you do that to that girl?"

Oh, hell, what happened on the show? Did the guest go apeshit or something? "Do what? I'm at the hospital with dad. He had a heart attack, man. He's gonna be okay, but if you're in town or close, I'm sure he'd love it if you could come see him."

Jacob quiets, and when he speaks up, he sounds more like his normal self. "Holy shit, man, is he okay?"

I sigh, purging some of the fear that's been roiling in my gut all night. "Yeah, it was some scary shit there for a bit, but he called in time. He knew right away something was wrong, so he got help within minutes. It was serious, but he's gonna be okay."

"I get that, and I don't mean to be insensitive, but I gotta ask. What about the show last night? You didn't air the recordings?"

"Recordings?" I ask, confused. "What recordings? I ran out the door as soon as Dad called. Figured Susannah would handle it."

I'm getting an ugly feeling in the pit of my stomach as the silence on the other end of the line stretches out, and I'm nervous as hell waiting for an answer. "Fuck, Derrick. Susannah, she played . . ."

"What?" I ask, nearly panic-stricken at this point. I don't need this shit. I so don't need this shit right now. "Just say it."

"She spent most of the first two hours playing recordings of you and Kat for the audience to comment on. It sounded like you were in the studio, talking with her, answering her questions, and you even laughed and said 'let's hear it.' Then, after that, it was you and Kat . . . uh, getting down and dirty."

"What are you talking about? Are you sure? Did you hear it yourself? How in the fuck are there even recordings of that?"

"You didn't record them? I mean, that doesn't sound like something you'd do, but how else?"

I feel the world start to spin, and I lean against my car, planting my hand on the roof to make sure I don't pass out. "No, I didn't record them. How bad was it?"

"It was bad. I'm not gonna repeat it all to you, but you should know, it was bad. I mean, I've seen pornos that had less explicit dialogue."

Oh, dear God. "What? How do those even exist? I didn't record them. I have to go, Jacob. I have to find Kat, find out what the fuck happened. Can you come to the hospital and sit with Dad for a little bit?"

"I'll be there this afternoon. The team's doing okay. I can take a day off for personal time. Hell, training staff keeps telling me to rest my shoulder anyway. I'm on my way, brother. Go get your woman and fix this. From what it sounds like, you might want a lawyer. If you do, I know a guy."

"Uh, right. We'll figure that out later though. Thanks, I appreciate it."

I hang up and run back upstairs to Dad's room, trying to figure out what to do as my mind races. Susannah could totally use sound bites of me on-air to make it sound like I was in the studio. We do that all the time for popular jokes so we can replay them and laugh at ourselves. But this is wholly different. She made it sound like I agreed with airing my own sex tapes, for fuck's sake. She might have ruined everything . . . with work, and more importantly, with Kat.

"Derrick?"

I stop, realizing I've been pacing the floor, and turn to see Dad. He's woken up, looking better than he did last night, but he's worried. "Everything okay?" I ask him.

He reaches over and uses the buttons on his bed to elevate himself to a near-seated position. "Son, you look worse than me, like the world just came crashing down on your head. What's going on? Besides the obvious."

I come over to his bed, feeling like I really shouldn't be burdening him. But looking in his eyes, I realize that maybe that's exactly what he needs right now. To not feel like a burden himself, but to be able to be that strong man who helped me so many times before in my life. "I don't know what happened, but I think my entire relationship with Kat just got really messed up last night."

"Kat's the young woman you told me about," Dad says, nodding. "The one you say you want to marry?"

I nod, swallowing. "And work, but I don't care about work . . . just Kat." I give him the fast and dirty of what I know, which admittedly, isn't much. I try to leave out some of the graphic details, as if it were just a little dirty talk. "And then last night, Susannah apparently aired some recordings of my chats with Kat. What the hell am I supposed to do?"

Dad nods, speaking slowly in that way he does when he's handing out his wisdom and wants to make sure you hear his best advice in your heart, not just your ears. "You love her?"

I nod. "Yes, of course. I love her so much."

"I know I raised you better than to disrespect any woman like that, so I won't even ask if you had anything to do with it."

It's a statement, but there's a threat in his tone and I can tell he's fishing for me to put his mind at ease. "Stay in bed, old man. I swear I had nothing to do with this. I'm just as horrified and pissed as she probably is. I never recorded any of it. How it got recorded, I have no idea."

He nods, his eyes flinty with furious anger and righteous determination. "Then you need to go fix this. I'll be fine right here in this bed. I ain't going nowhere. Make your mom and me proud, Son, just like you always have."

"Thanks, Dad. Jacob said he'd stop by this afternoon though. He's going to take a personal day and sit with you as long as you want."

I lean in and give him another hug, knowing that I could've lost him yesterday, and I'm so damn thankful for the man he is and the man he taught me to be. Whatever the hell just happened, I'm going full-throttle to fix this shit.

CHAPTER 24

KAT

The knock on the door comes at a time when the last thing I want is more people around, but Elise is having nothing of it. "I already called them. Jess heard the show anyway, so she's not going to take no for an answer."

She's right. My mother and sister come into Elise's apartment like a pair of Tasmanian devils, whirling around and searching for me. "Kat?" Jess says before seeing me curled up on the couch underneath Elise's comforter. "There you are. Good. I've got that ginger beer you like, those flannel pajamas from your third drawer down in your dresser, and my samurai sword."

"You've got a samurai sword?" Elise asks.

"Not really, but I do have a big ass chef's knife back at home if I need to go get it. Just as good," Jess replies.

"That won't be necessary," I grumble, smiling some at her being so protective. "But thanks for the PJs."

"Of course," she says, handing me the threadbare but much-loved Elmo pajamas.

"Sis, if I give one of my clients a call, he knows some guys who could pay him a little visit and rough him up."

"No," I mumble around a mouthful of ice cream. "Please, no."

"Yeah, you're probably right," she says, sipping at the ginger beer, "but if you don't rip him a new one, I'm doing it for you!

Mom butts in, getting down to business. "Katrina, I don't want to put you down, but have you thought that maybe there's an explanation for this?" she asks. "I mean, I've never talked to Derrick, but from everything you said, he seems like a good man. While his show's not *Mr. Roger's Neighborhood*, why would he do it? Seems like he'd be just as embarrassed as you. I can't imagine his employers liked that going on the air either."

"Wait, you listen to *The Love Whisperer*?" Elise asks. "Oh, my God, I'm so glad my parents don't have satellite radio."

"Mom," Jess says, shaking her head. "Mom, I love you, but even I've got to say you're being a little too naive here. Come on, the recordings were phone calls and video chats, not police wiretapping or some spy cam action."

"But Derrick broke the law if he recorded them, right?" Mom asks. "I mean, you can't just broadcast someone's sex life without their consent, can you?"

Elise shrugs. "Gray area right now. Recording a call one-sided is legal in this state. Trust me, I know all about that one with my job. Beats me if the content matters."

"Besides," Elise says, "he gave his permission to broadcast. Kat, I know you missed that part, but I heard it."

I sniffle, tears threatening again. "Can we just change the subject, please?"

Mom nods, hugging me again. "I'm so sorry, baby."

I lean against her, drawing scant comfort from her presence, but at least there's something. "Remember when you said that even with the pain of it ending with Dad, you wouldn't trade the good days?"

"Yeah."

"Well, I would," I declare miserably. "It's not just the good days. It was the hope that maybe I was wrong, that I could have what you and Jess have. This isn't about our being over. This is about my hope being dashed beyond recognition. I'm not doing this anymore, ever again."

Before anyone can say anything, I get up, wrapping up in Elise's comforter and shuffling off to the bedroom. She's got a big bed, and between the comforter I've already got and her fluffy blanket she's got here, I quickly get a good misery nest wormed up and snuggle in deep, hiding in my cocoon. I have a half-formed thought that instead of eventually emerging a beautiful butterfly, I'm going to come out of this a hardened bitch. But maybe that's safer in the end.

There's no way I'm going to sleep, even if I couldn't still hear them talking.

"Has she even talked to him yet?" Jess asks Elise quietly. "I mean, all jokes aside, I'd like to hear this excuse."

"Maybe screaming and cussing him out would help?" Elise asks. "I mean, it couldn't hurt, right? Sorry, she hasn't even turned her phone back on after that call to him when she realized that he ignored her."

Mom sounds bleakly hopeful. "Maybe he's called by now?"

Elise lowers her voice, but I can still hear her. "No. I turned it back on when I forced her into the shower this morning. He still hadn't called and I deleted a bunch of texts from people at work who heard about it. Oh, and Kevin sent her stupid shit that makes me want to slap his fucking face. I'm planning on dealing with his ass soon enough."

I hear my Mom's gasp, and while I'm pissed that Elise screwed with my phone, she's got a good heart. She's right. I should have checked for Derrick to call back. "I never liked that weasel," Mom says.

I groan and roll over. Everyone knows I'll never be able to show my face at work again. Fuckstick Kevin even thinks he's worthy of my time now. I may be embarrassed as hell, but I'm never falling that far off the scale again.

Nope, just gonna stay alone, me and my lines of code that are predictable and reliable, unlike men. Maybe get that dog after all.

There's a buzzing sound, and then Elise's voice. "Ugh . . . They're not being completely rude like Kevin, but I'm going to have to teach some of her co-workers a lesson too. I'm gonna turn this back off for now. She doesn't need any of this shit right now."

I bury my head underneath the dual comforters, hoping to drown out the noise. Maybe eventually, I'll get to sleep and wake up to find out this was all just a nightmare.

"*ey, this is Kat. I'm busy so leave a message at the beep.*"

I slam my fist down on the passenger seat of my car, growling. Each time I call, it goes straight to voicemail.

I went to her apartment, banging on her door loudly enough for one of the neighbors to stick their head out and tell me to shut the fuck up or else they'd call the cops. Yeah, that's the last fucking thing I need.

Knowing I've got at least one more shitstorm I've got to deal with, I head into work. Walking through the small reception area, I know I've got laser beams shooting from my eyes and fire drifting from my nostrils as two of the front staff cower from my glare. They normally are pretty nice. I've shot the shit with them plenty of times. Not today.

"What the fuck was that last night?" I explode as I storm into my office to see Susannah seated at the work table, her little clipboard arranged perfectly in front of her. "What was going through your fucking head?"

She taps her clipboard with a pen, looking up with an expression on her face of total and complete calm. "Nice to see you too. I covered for you when you bailed and didn't answer your phone the dozens of times I called to find out where the fuck you went. You've been mentally absent for weeks now, Derrick. I saved your ass and the show, just like I always do. You're welcome, by the way."

I stop in my tracks, dumbfounded. Not sure what excuse I was expecting, but it damn sure wasn't that. "Covered for me? You should've just played an old show. How the hell did you get those recordings?"

My yelling is attracting an audience, people poking their heads out and freezing in the hallway to watch the show through the glass door, but I'm way beyond caring.

Susannah, on the other hand, is playing it cool as a cucumber. "You're the one having phone sex in the middle of the studio. I just aired them. I could've filed suit for creating a hostile work environment, you know. I did you a favor."

The door to my office opens and the station manager, Quincy Kilborne, comes in. A long-time veteran of the radio game, Quincy's been a strong supporter of my show from the beginning. Today, though, he looks pissed.

"What the hell's going on in here? Why are you two yelling at each other when the show starts in an hour?" He crosses his arms over his chest, looking at us like we're misbehaving children.

I swallow back an eruption of rage and stifle my voice. "Susannah played recordings of my private conversations on air. Last night's show . . . I didn't make those recordings, and I damn sure didn't give my permission to air them."

"Is that true?" Quincy asks, raising an eyebrow. "Let's be clear—we're talking about a possible felony accusation here. What happened yesterday?"

"He . . ." Susannah says, her mask of self-control faltering as she stutters slightly. "You heard it. I played it. He gave permission to play those recordings. Go back and listen. You'll see."

Quincy looks at me, but before he can even ask, I'm all over it. "Bullshit. That was an edited soundbite. The whole damn thing was edited. I left during the pre-show meeting yesterday in a hurry."

"Yeah," Susannah scoffs. "Running off to go see your fuck buddy instead of working, just like you have every day for weeks. So typical of you these days. I've been covering for you every damn day."

Quincy looks between us, and I can see it in his eyes that he doesn't believe Susannah either. Who would? I fucking hope Kat doesn't. "I went to the hospital to see my dad," I explain. "He had a heart attack. He called during the pre-show and I ran to meet the ambulance at the hospital. I didn't have time to explain. I was in a panic. Call the damn hospital. I spent the whole night there. Fire me if you need to for bailing, but the bigger problem here is how Susannah got the recordings. Those were private."

Susannah starts to fidget in her seat for a few moments. "Well?" Quincy asks. "How did you get those conversations?"

"I recorded them!" Susannah finally explodes after seeing the silent act isn't going to work. "You're sitting there in the studio every night, just winging the whole damn thing by the seat of your Jockeys while I'm prepping the music, the emails, the next caller. Meanwhile, you're fucking off talking to your latest and greatest. Fuck that. We had something good going when you were single, or at least you were focused on the show and helping me make it great."

"Wait . . . but how's that possible?" I fume back. "And yeah, I admitted to you that I wasn't giving a hundred percent. I apologized for that. But I was still pulling my weight. The show's been doing fine and that's no fucking excuse!"

"Because I'm picking up your slack!" Susannah screams. "I'm the one who sets up the callers. I'm the one who does the music. I'm the one who chooses the emails. I'm the one who does every *fucking* thing this show needs except, of course, milk your fucking cock when you want it milked! And for that, what do I get? You texting your goddamn girlfriend while I'm busting my ass!"

"Susannah, I already apologized—"

"Stick your apology up your ass!" Susannah screams. "I do all the work, and somehow, you get to waltz in, drop some Barry White smooth tones and lame advice, and you get all the credit. The damn show's even named after you. I'm not even a fucking side note. I'm the one carrying the whole show on my shoulders, working to get us into syndication and studio deals, and I barely get anything! ANYTHING!"

"What you do get is invading my privacy," I seethe, my voice dropping to an enraged calmness. "I talked it over with a friend and pulled the archives of the show. That wasn't just phone calls, and it wasn't stuff I did in the studio. At least three of the clips you played were things I did in my apartment, on *my* time. How the fuck did you do that?"

Susannah says nothing, crossing her arms over her chest. "I want a lawyer. This is sexual harassment."

Quincy speaks up. "If anyone has a case for harassment, it's Derrick. Can I see your phone?" he says, nodding to me.

I'm hesitant for a second, considering what's just happened with my phone, but I hand it over and he starts tapping at the screen. He hands it to me, showing me the task manager with something running in the background I've never installed. "Uh-huh . . . thought so. Wouldn't have had a damn clue how to check this, but I saw it on TV the other day. She must've installed this on your phone somehow."

"What—" I start, taking the phone in trembling fingers before remembering. "That time you were screwing with my phone, when I stepped out to take a piss."

Susannah shrugs, finally deciding that offense is the best defense. "I had to do it. I just wanted to see what I was up against. I needed you here with me, and knowledge is power. If I knew what you were doing, I could cover for you, work with you, maybe get you to see the light that you don't need her and she's screwing everything up. We're on the cusp of greatness here, and it's everything I've worked so hard for. And you're not only letting it slip away, you're walking away for some damn pussy. After I listened to a few of the conversations, I thought it would be good for the show. Hell, it got me hot and I don't even think of you that way. If she got mad and dumped you, then you'd re-focus on the show and we could go back to how it was before. Win-win."

"Win-win? Like before?" I ask, staring at my phone. My hands are shaking so hard I can barely control myself, and the world narrows to a single black tunnel as I stare at the welcome screen for the spyware. My fist clenches, squeezing the sides of my phone until there's a cracking sound, and suddenly, my phone's screen goes black. I drop the wreck on the table and look up at Susannah. "How on earth could it be like before after what you did?"

Quincy doesn't let her respond. "Susannah, you're fired. Gather your shit and get out."

"You'll be hearing from my lawyer," Susannah growls. "You hear me? I'm gonna own this station by the time I'm done with you."

"Ms. Jameson, you're going to be lucky if you don't serve time. I'm reporting your actions to the police even if Mr. King here doesn't. You're not walking away from this. Your actions have risked the station and the show. I'll call security to escort you out."

Instead of waiting, Susannah storms out, kicking my office door open before screaming in rage as she heads down the hallway. In the strange silence that follows, I turn to Quincy, who's watching my office door close on its pneumatic hinge. "I'm sorry about all—" I attempt.

"Forget it," Quincy says. "I actually listen to the show, Derrick. Not as a boss, but just as a listener. Maybe she was carrying more load behind the scenes, but the success of the show on-air is about you, and there *has* been something different lately. You seem *happier* on-air, like you believe the happily ever after shit you peddle, and it gives us all hope, even my crusty old soul. Maybe we need to get you an assistant for the prep and a co-host for on-air, but regardless, what Susannah did is about as wrong as it gets."

I let out a relieved sigh, realizing I'm not fired too. "What about the show? We *had* to be breaking some rules last night."

Quincy shrugs. "We'll probably catch some shit, but as long as we don't pull anything like that again, we'll be fine."

"And the show tonight?" I ask, looking at my cracked phone. "I really shouldn't have done that . . . how the hell am I going to call Kat now?"

"Go get a new phone. If she meant that much to you, you have to know her number," Quincy says. "As for your show, we'll cue up one of the recorded ones. Take a few days, get yourself together, and we'll line up some help for you. I know we've got some producers in-house who would give anything to work with the Love Whisperer, and I'll put out some feelers for a co-host. Think of it this way, you've got a hell of an opening monologue to do if you want."

"Yeah . . ." I mumble, not sure what else to say. "Quincy, I know I should start helping with everything now, but—"

"Go handle your business," he says, patting me on the shoulder. "We got this."

I think. How am I supposed to reach out to Kat when she isn't answering me and I don't know where she is? Suddenly, it hits me, and I look Quincy in the eye. "Actually, I need to get on the radio tonight. At least that first half hour or so. Think Phil would mind being my producer tonight?"

He gives me a small, tight smile. "Hell, if he can't, I think I can still run a basic board. Just don't ask me to do any digital magic."

CHAPTER 26

KAT

I'm lying on the couch, trying to ignore the pain inside me by shooting balloons with monkeys on Elise's laptop when she comes in, carrying her phone. "Kat!"

"What?" I mutter, watching as a giant black blimp appears on screen. How appropriate. It fits my mood.

"Kat, you gotta listen to this," Elise says, dropping her phone into her stereo system. "Derrick's on!"

"You know I don't want to hear—" I start to shoot back, but before I can, Derrick's voice fills the room. It's raw, different from anything I've ever heard on the radio before. No, I've heard this voice . . . but only when he's just talking to me. I close my mouth, listening to every word.

"Okay, that was our opening break . . . Toni Braxton's Another Sad Love Song," Derrick says. *"Now normally, I'd start off*

the show with an introduction, a few laughs, maybe a little innuendo to get things rolling. But right now . . . well, this isn't The Love Whisperer talking. For those of you who are looking for some advice, maybe something closer to what we normally do here, tune in next hour. This hour, this is just me . . . plain ol' Derrick King trying to fix something that happened last night."

"You see," Derrick continues, *"last night was something that I never planned. Those of you who tuned in heard me give permission for certain racy recordings to be played on the air. Let me be clear. At no time did I authorize that. Folks, I didn't even know I was being recorded. What you heard last night were the highly edited versions of private conversations between me and the woman I love more deeply than I can ever say."*

"Do you believe him?" Elise asks.

"Shh!"

I turn my attention back as Derrick keeps going. *"I was betrayed by a now former coworker who put spyware on my phone when I wasn't looking. This person, and I'm not naming names due to pending legal action, but this person then took intimate private phone calls and video chats and spliced them together to create what she wanted. Fuck it, let's be plain. Who knows how many people heard it live? No need to beat around the bush. Kat, I didn't know about the recordings. I left the studio yesterday because my dad's in the hospital. What happened last night, I had no part in. Last night, I missed your phone call because I left my phone in my car when I rushed into the ER. I damn-near puked when I talked to Jacob this morning and he told me what had happened. I . . . I'm sorry."*

I stand up, walking toward the radio. "Derrick . . ."

I can hear the honesty in his voice, the raspiness as he speaks. *"Kat, I never wanted to hurt you. You've been through so much, and all I wanted in our lives was to keep making you happy. You've told me so many things, and I'd never do what happened last night even to an enemy . . . let alone to the woman I love. Please, I know you're angry. I'm angry too. Call me. I sorta broke my phone when I found out about the software, but they got me a new one and it's clean, I promise. Same number. It's sitting here in front of me. If you don't want to do that, call the show. I'll put the whole damn rest of the show on a mixtape if I need to. I love you, Kat. Call me."*

"I need to go to him," I say, turning to Elise. "I don't want to do this over the phone. I have to look him in the eye."

"Not like that, you aren't," Elise says with a tiny smile. "No offense, babe, but you smell like stale wine, along with a shitload of sweat and other general yuckiness. And you're still in your pajamas."

I look down and pull my pajama top off. Elmo drops to the floor, and I rush to the shower. "Lend me some clothes!"

"Got some sweats . . . not much else for this weather. You're too damn short!" Elise calls from her bedroom. "Good enough?"

"Good enough!" I say, scrubbing quickly. I hit the major areas and am jogging out the door exactly six minutes later, Elise's phone still broadcasting Derrick's voice.

"Folks, to everyone listening, I have this advice for you. Check your computers. Check your phones. What happened to me . . . well, I didn't even know spyware like that existed. It's invisible and they don't even need your phone password to install it, just your number. But you see, even knowing that, I don't regret having phone sex with a woman I care deeply for. I don't regret the video chats either. I do regret that what was loving and private between us was broadcast by someone jealous of my position on this show. I do regret that my sweet Kat, who is one of the kindest, most precious people in the world, was made to sound like something she's not through the magic of sound editing. Guys, you never heard the important parts of our calls. You didn't get to hear that, in between the sexy playful talk, we exchanged words of love, of commitment. You never got to listen as she joked with me about our breaking the closet barrier right after that last sound clip where she called out my name. So protect yourselves. If you want to have phone sex, that's fine. You want to naughty chat, that's fine too. But protect yourself."

We peel ass through the city, heading toward the studio. When I get there, Elise struggles to keep up with me as I rush in the front door. "Where's Derrick?"

"I'm sorry," the receptionist says, "but Mr. King—"

"Goddammit, I'm Kat!" I yell. "His Kitty Kat!"

The receptionist's eyes flash in recognition, and without another word, she leads me down a short hallway to a studio, where she knocks on the door. "Derrick? You have a visitor."

I step into the studio, where Derrick cuts off his most recent monologue mid-sentence. "Excuse me, everyone, we're going to cut to some music. Uh . . . Kat's here. Wish me luck."

In another connecting booth, an older, slightly balding man in a suit throws some switches, and Nirvana's *All Apologies* starts playing.

"Kat," Derrick says, but before he can say anything more, I collapse into his arms, holding him close. "I'm so sorry."

"I'm so sorry too." I cry, burying my nose in his shirt. He smells a little funky too and is going on a couple of days' growth of untrimmed beard for sure. Somehow, those two little details tell me that everything he's said is the truth.

Derrick holds me close, "Kat, I know I hurt you—"

"No . . . *she* did," I reply, looking up at him. "Yeah, I was furious at you last night, but I should've trusted that something wasn't right. It wasn't like you to do that, but it was hard to trust my heart over my own ears. It brought up old issues and insecurities, and I just fell back into that dark place so fast, but it was so much worse because it was you and I love you so damn much. But I heard you just now. It wasn't your fault and we were both hurt by her actions. It wasn't our fault. Where is she?"

"I love you too, Kat. She's been fired, and both me and the station have retained lawyers," Derrick says. "Illegal wire-tapping, invasion of privacy, I don't fucking know what you call it but it's damn sure illegal. She'll never work in radio again and might do jail time. Quincy, the station manager, says he'll back me in whatever I want to do."

I nod and settle deeper into Derrick's arms. "Okay, we'll deal with that. But I've got more important things to worry about now that I know it wasn't you."

"Like what?" Derrick asks, and I reach up, cupping his face.

"Tell me what happened with your dad." my eyes are imploring here, the concern shining genuinely.

Derrick nods. "He's gonna be okay, but he had a major heart attack and it was pretty serious for a while last night at the hospital. It was scary." He shrugs as if even saying he was scared isn't okay, but it's obviously the truth. "He's my dad, and I thought I was gonna lose him."

I wrap both arms around his waist, hugging him tight. "I'm so sorry, Derrick. I know that must have been terrifying. I'm glad he's gonna be okay though."

He smiles a bit, his eyes crinkling at the corners. "I told him about you, by the way."

The fact that he was thinking about me at all with everything going on with his dad warms my heart. He was lost last night, unaware of the storm raging on the radio and in my heart, but even in his dark moment, he thought to tell his dad about me. "Really?"

He kisses the top of my head, "He can't wait to meet you."

He turns to the producer, who gives him a single finger. "One minute, then let's get out of here."

I wait as Derrick slides behind the mic, leaning forward and looking at me, his eyes gleaming. As soon as the little red light on his board lights up, he speaks. "Love Whisperer fans, there are times when I don't know if I'm reaching anyone with my show. But tonight, I know the most important person was listening, and I reached her, and she reached right back out to me. So, we're going to flip the show over to one of our *Best of the Love Whisperer* shows, because I'm taking the love of my life to meet my father. Until next time."

Derrick tosses the producer a wave as another song starts up. I have to laugh as Smashmouth's version of *I'm A Believer* starts playing. As we walk out, I see the receptionist give a little fist pump. "You know all of your fans are going to want to find out the details now."

"They're going to have to wait," Derrick says. "Our business is our business."

"Actually, I was thinking . . . It might do us both some good to get in front of the gossip and address it, maybe do a bit of damage control on air with a special guest . . . chick named Katrina. Might help your reputations, the show, and the station. Just a thought."

"I'll think about it," Derrick growls, pulling me close. I wrap my arms around his neck as he lifts me in his powerful arms. Our lips touch, and in the first tender caress of his lips, I know all I need to know.

His tongue strokes over my bottom lip and I open up to him, moaning softly as his hands pull me against his body. I'm exhausted. I barely slept last night, but it doesn't matter as I press my body against his. I feel a tingle deep inside, but it's more than just desire . . . it's my heart.

"I love you," Derrick whispers when we part to breathe.

"I know, and me too," I reply. "Come on, take me to see your dad."

As soon as we make it to the car, Derrick roughly pulls me into his lap, his warm kiss taking the breath out of my lungs in the chilly night air. I moan as he brings a hand up to cup my breast, squeezing gently as he kisses and nibbles down the line of my neck. I reach between us to trace the line of his growing cock in his jeans. Panting, Derrick breaks our kiss, pulling back to rest his forehead against mine. "Make no mistake, you are mine, Kat. Now and always."

I nod, biting my lip. "Yours forever. And you're mine too."

He presses one more quick kiss to my lips in agreement. "Yours too."

It seems to be the reassurance we both need, and he works to calm the heated tension sparking in the confined space of the car. "Can't wait to finish this. But first, I've got an old man for you to meet."

*I*t's a normal-looking hospital room, but the giant of a man sitting in the chair next to the bed certainly isn't. "Well, now, we weren't expecting you two to stop by," Jacob says as he gets up. "I figured you'd be at home."

"Yeah, well," Derrick says, scratching at his head, "Dad,

this is Katrina Snow, my girlfriend. Kat, this is my father, Daniel King."

Daniel sits up, smiling a little, and I see he's wearing a t-shirt from Jacob's team. "Check out the new swag," he says with a grin before looking at me. "So you're the one who's making my boy see stars?"

I know I'm blushing, but I step forward, shaking his hand. "Maybe so, sir, but he's the one making me believe in fairy tales, that sometimes they do come true, even if they're a bit messy."

"Not messy," Jacob says, grinning. "Just sometimes a little . . . dirty. And there ain't a thing wrong with that."

I smile a bit uncomfortably. It's more than a little weird to know that my boyfriend's father and friends have probably heard me say things I wouldn't want a soul on Earth to hear. I guess I'll have to get used to it for a bit until all of this dies down. "That's true. So, are we still on for the game?"

"Actually, I had to turn in the box tickets to get the day off," Jacob admits, "but we've got one more home game before the playoffs. It's going to be chilly, and I'll be honest, you'll have to share the box with some other player's guests, but it's a big box. What do you say?"

"I say this old man will be ready for it, but only if you quit hovering about. Go on, you all get out of here," Daniel says, chuckling. "Leave me to heal and rest. And Jacob? Make damn sure you get into the playoffs."

"You heard the man," Derrick says, taking my hand. "Dad, we'll come by sometime tomorrow."

We leave, and at the elevator, Jacob wraps his arms around me, nearly crushing me in a bear hug. "I'm happy for you. Take care of him, okay?"

"I will," I groan, trying to hug him back but nowhere able to get my arms around his enormous torso. Still, I pound him on the back as best I can, touched that for such a fearsome football gladiator, he's a big teddy bear inside.

CHAPTER 27

*M*y hands are trembling with excitement as I turn my key in the lock to my place, letting me lead Kat inside. "Kat . . ."

She turns to me, placing a finger over my lips and looking at me saucily. "Derrick, fuck me. Make love to me. That's all I need." And she walks inside, heading for my bedroom. "Make me feel like the woman that you've reminded me I am."

I can't really argue, so I just watch in utter fascination as she sways her way across my living room, an utter sex goddess in oversized sweatpants. But it's not the clothes. It's the aura of sensuality that just seems to exude from every pore in her body. She's the total package, the one I've always known was out there for me somewhere—sexy, intelligent, sweet, and overall, an amazing woman. Maybe I sensed all that way back on our first phone conversation on the air somehow, and I just didn't realize what it meant yet. But I do now.

"Wait," I say, locking my door behind me. "Not the bedroom."

"Oh?" Kat asks, turning to me. "Why not?"

"Because I'm pretty funky . . . I was thinking the shower?" I ask in reply. "That is . . . if you don't mind my washing you down so I can dirty you up?"

"Well, I had a shower just before coming to the studio," she teases lightly before continuing with a bit of promise, "but my hair could use a good washing. By your hands, of course."

The idea of running my fingers through Kat's honey tresses suddenly has my cock aching, and I hurry to follow her into the bathroom. It's one of the benefits of my not being a sports reporter anymore. I've been able to upgrade to an apartment with one sweet bathroom that has a large glass shower stall lined in black marble. Kat's been here before, of course, but she takes a moment to admire the room as she reaches for the hem of her shirt. "Nice choice."

"For what?" I ask, regaining some of my control and pulling her toward me.

Kat teases, reaching down and cupping my cock through my jeans again, and the response is immediate, my body already warmed up from before. "I was thinking this is a nice choice for the first place I want you to really fuck me. Fill me with that big cock and come inside me."

I swallow, looking into her eyes. "Kat, before this all happened, I was thinking about—"

"The same thing I was thinking about. And when the time's right, we'll get there. My answer's going to be the same as before all of this. Yes."

Her words are all I need as I crush her lips in a searing kiss, tearing at her clothes as we undress each other. I say a silent prayer of thanks for sweatpants. They're so easy to peel off as I kneel in front of her, kissing at the soft skin of her belly just above the line of her panties, then tugging them down to look at her beautiful pussy.

I see her sweet clit start to pulse in time with her heart-beat, needy for attention. "Tell me, Kat."

She eases her legs a little farther apart, giving me more of a peek at her sexy center but still not saying what I need to hear.

Kat runs her fingers through my hair, pulling the strands back and making me growl. I inhale her, memorizing every nuance to her natural perfume before lifting my eyes toward her without moving away from her sexy cunt. There's a warning in my voice. "Kat . . ."

She smirks, but the quiver in her thighs under my hands belies her flirty tone. "I think I like being in charge a little."

"And you can be, from time to time," I joke, kissing lower, deciding that if she wants to tease me by not letting me have my way with her dripping pussy, I can torment her right back and make it impossible for her to deny me.

I nip at her stomach, and she gasps, relenting with a moan. "Eat my pussy, Derrick. Do it for me."

265

Permission granted, I stroke my tongue between her slick pussy lips, the soft and silky folds parting under my tongue. I shiver as I eat her slowly, relishing every sweet drop of her arousal.

"Oh, fuck, Derrick, that's it. You make me feel so good, don't stop, please. Suck my clit. Hard."

I want to give her everything—what she asks for, what she needs, and what she doesn't even know she needs. I'll give her all that I am, all that I have, knowing that she'll do the same for me. So I cup her ass, bringing her in close to lick up and down her slit, circling her clit slowly before drawing it in. I suck her hard nub and thrash my tongue across it at the same time, giving her no mercy. Kat's hips shiver and her thighs clench under my hands. "Derrick, fuck, I'm gonna—"

"Come for me, my love," I rasp, looking up at her with devotion. "Come all over my face."

I dive back in, hungry to taste her orgasm. She cries out as a gush of wetness covers my face and chin, and I feel reborn, connected in a way that we've never been before. Kat pulls on my hair, pushing me in deeper and deeper until her orgasm finally ebbs.

"That's the warm-up?" Kat asks shakily as she steps back, stepping the rest of the way out of her clothes. She pulls her shirt off while I quickly strip out of my clothes, getting into the shower and starting the water. Kat watches, her naked body glowing under the lights, smirking. "Warm enough?"

"I'll make sure it is," I promise her, holding open the glass door for her. As soon as she's in, I consume her, kissing her hard and pressing her lush body against the cool glass. My cock is throbbing, mashed between our bodies as the steamy air fills the shower.

Nibbling down Kat's neck, I bring my hand up, massaging and pinching her nipple as she moans in my ear. "Mmm, your turn to be in charge now?"

"You know damn well it is," I growl, loving the look in her eyes. It's the look of the future, the rest of my life, and I can't wait for it. Love, intense and overflowing . . . taking turns 'being in charge' while the whole time, things are really a team effort. "You're my woman. Forever."

"Forever," Kat repeats, reaching down and grasping my rock-hard cock in her soft hand. The water sprays over my back and shoulders as we kiss, her hand slowly stroking my shaft while I run my thumb over her nipple, teasing and pinching it until it's diamond hard. Kat's whimpers tell me how good it feels, and I turn her around, massaging her breasts while lavishing her neck with kisses. "Mmm . . . that's wonderful."

"Just getting started," I rasp in her ear, running my hand down to cup her pussy. She's already recovered, her pussy clenching around my two fingers as I slide them in, pumping them in and out slowly. Finally, I withdraw them and line myself up. "You ready?"

"Make me yours forever," Kat moans. I spread my legs, lowering myself enough that I can slide the head of my cock between her legs. With one long, slow thrust, I slide inside her, both of us groaning as every inch of my cock stretches her. Once I'm balls-deep, I still to let her adjust, enjoying the sensation of her wet heat wrapped around my bare cock, nothing coming between the love and trust we share. Kat's deep gasp comes from the depths of her soul, and I feel the same way as I join with her . . . the last woman I'll ever join with.

I push in deeper, bottoming out inside her, both of us gasping again as her pussy squeezes me tightly, massaging my shaft. Kat turns her head to look into my eyes, her open mouth trembling. "I love you."

"I love you, too," I answer. The pleasure is too much and instinct takes over. I pull back and thrust deep into her again, grinning. "Forever."

Kat nods, and we let our bodies tell us what to do. My cock strokes in and out as my hands roam her body, memorizing every inch of her soft skin. "Your sweet pussy feels so good around me. God, Kat, I want to be inside you all the time." Her soft mewls echo in the shower, encouraging me.

I can't go too fast, the open-legged stance I have to take keeping me from jackhammering her, but that's okay. I pound into her, watching her ass shake from the force of each driving plunge. "You like that, Kat?"

She nods, and I do it again and again, grabbing handfuls of her hips for leverage. "Me too. I'm gonna pound your pussy and remind you that you're mine." The warm water cascades down our bodies, the slap of my hips against Kat's ass beating in time with our rising heartrates as we caress each other.

Kat presses her hands against the glass wall, urging me on, and I lift her onto her tiptoes, my fingers digging into the soft flesh of her hips to keep her there. "Yes, fuck me, Derrick. Give it all to me. Fill me up."

I speed up, her voice sending me into overdrive. My pulse hammers in my veins, and my eyes fix at the beautiful, sexy sight of my cock pumping in and out of Kat's pussy, squeezed and caressed. My nerves are on fire, and her pussy's clenching around me with every hard stroke, begging me to stay inside while at the same time begging for release. I go faster, as hard as I dare until I feel it. "Take it all!"

My orgasm hits me like an uppercut to the chin. Stars shoot across my vision, and I explode, filling Kat with everything that I have.

My arms tremble, and in the dim recesses of my mind, I hear Kat cry out too, her pussy clamping down on me as we stay frozen. I think we'd be there forever if it wasn't for the sudden cramp in my hamstring that pulls me back from this eternity, and I pull out, panting and laughing at the same time.

"What is it?" Kat asks, turning around to see me bending over, stretching my leg.

"Cramp," I hiss, my cock slowly wilting as the now cool water splashes down my back and ass to drip off my balls. "We need to put a step in here if this is going to be a regular thing."

Kat blinks, then chuckles as she raises an eyebrow. "Is that your way of saying I'm short?"

I laugh lightly, pulling her into me, our bodies slippery and slick against each other. "Of course not. You're not short, just fun-sized. You just need a little lift so I can *really* give it to you like I want."

"Is that your way of inviting me to move in?" She's smiling, but I can see the smallest hint of uncertainty in the depths of her eyes.

"As soon as you can break your lease," I reply. "I want to go to sleep with you in my arms, wake up with you in our bed, and spend every day together. I'm ready when you are."

CHAPTER 28

KAT

he box is busy, but Jacob had warned us of that. The team's facing their last home game, and it's a must-win situation, according to Derrick, so a lot of the players used their allotments for this game, resulting in a box filled with a dozen or more people. Thankfully, all of them are family of Jacob's teammates. It makes things . . . interesting.

"So, you're the one who wrote that app?" one of them, a bubbly, curly-haired woman named Rachel, asks. "I just downloaded that last week. Girl, let me tell you, that has been a godsend. I've been able to do so much more, and Jerry's been happier too! He's been able to see that I'm not just wasting time being some WAG. Now, let me ask you . . . think you can write a day trading app?"

I chuckle, sipping the flute of champagne that comes with the box seats. "I could, but I doubt it'd be better than what's out there. Why?"

"A deal Jerry and I have. Each season, we take one game check each and we get to invest it the way we want. He does it in real estate, and he's made some good deals. But I do day trading. I'd like to squeeze out another three percent."

"Why's that?" I ask, trying not to let on that her blithely playing with thousands of dollars makes me a little twitchy. I mean, my job doesn't have me scraping to pay the bills anymore . . . but it's not like I can drop money like this on a whim.

"Whoever gets a bigger return gets to be in charge of our anniversary celebration," Rachel says, giggling. "Last year, I won, and I think Jerry liked it. So this year, I want to go whole hog. Leather, chains . . . he might be a football stud, but if I can get that three percent, he's gonna be my little bitch."

I gawk, then laugh. "You should talk to my boyfriend, Derrick. He'll—"

"Oh, we all know Derrick," Rachel whispers. "Half the players and wives listen in. Congrats. That was one hell of an interview, girl! Now come on, game's about to start."

We sit down, me in between Derrick and Daniel, who insists that I call him Dad. He's still recovering from his heart attack, but he looks a lot stronger in just a few weeks, and we make up for his lack of strength with our own cheering.

"You still don't have any clue what's going on, do you?" Derrick whispers as he leans over during one of the time-outs. "Didn't get to read that book?"

"I tried, but I've been kinda busy," I deadpan. We both chuckle, although it's not too dark a chuckle.

It hasn't been very easy, dealing with the aftermath. So far, Susannah's trying to cover her ass, being as 'cooperative' as possible in the hopes that Derrick and I don't go after her with a civil suit. But that's not the hard part. While the Monday show after our getting back together had plenty of respectful, supportive callers and guests, Derrick's had to deal with a little backlash from some of his female fans.

There were a few emails from pearl-clutchers who didn't appreciate that he called me his 'dirty slut' in our phone sex recordings, but he handled it with his usual aplomb that what consenting adults do and say in the privacy of their own sex lives isn't up for judgement by folks who aren't involved. I cringed a little when he reminded everyone that he hadn't invited them into his dirty talk, but it seemed to shut the critics up.

The other backlash was related to his appeal, at least partially, being because of his apparent 'availability,' and he shattered quite a few fantasies when his girlfriend came on the air and we publicly said we love each other and were moving in together.

We've both been a little bitter about people feeling entitled to an opinion about something that's none of their business, and we've both dealt with trolls and perverts who've sent in daily requests to 'see the Kitty Kat,' along with their 'suggestions' as to what they'd do with me.

Quincy, Derrick's manager, has been pretty supportive.

He worked with Derrick to make sure that the new producer, a married woman named Janet, is totally professional, and he's done a good job of screening out the assholes and opportunists who've applied to be the new co-host.

"Hey," Derrick asks, leaning over, "you okay? Looked lost in thought. They still giving you problems at work?"

I shake my head, smiling. "No. A few slimy comments, but nothing I can't handle. If anything, your show's actually become a big hit around the office."

Derrick laughs, our laughter being drowned out as a massive roar goes through the stadium. I look out, and most of the cheering fans are for the away team, so I guess it was bad for us. "Uh, what happened?"

"Big punt return," Daniel says, his eyes fixed on the field. "I'd say we're going to give up at least a field goal. They've got first and ten on the twelve yard line."

I nod, half of what 'Dad' just said going straight over my head, but I can see the position on the field, and I make sure to watch as the defense lines up. I memorized Jacob's number, and I jump out of my seat cheering as number ninety-two bum rushes through and tackles the quarterback for a big loss. "Go, Jacob!"

"Big sack!" Dad cheers, grinning. "That's the way to collapse the pocket!"

"Huh?" I ask, glancing at Derrick. "Uhm, I'm just glad I remembered who the quarterback was."

Derrick grins, leaning in. "I think after my lesson, you can at least remember that much."

I blush, my body tingling as I think of our last-minute 'football lesson' that turned into sex after Derrick had me bend over as the 'center' and he got behind me for the snap. He gave my right cheek a swift smack and then smoothed it over with a grabbing caress, and feeling his strong hands on my ass triggered a need for something more than football knowledge. Apparently, it was the same thing for him because we almost ended up late to pick up Daniel after finishing up our 'lesson'. "I hope the real center and quarterback don't end up like that."

"Who knows?" Derrick chuckles. "Come on, let's keep watching."

The game's first half goes well, and when halftime comes, it's still close. "Time for some snacks," Daniel says, getting up. Because of his heart attack, his diet is much stricter than it used to be, and he's not allowed alcohol or fatty foods, but today, he said he was taking a very rare exception and splurged on a small plateful of buffalo wings already. "I'm gonna grab some bites from the veggie tray. You guys want anything?"

"They got any nachos back there?" Derrick asks. "Feeling like cheese."

Daniel nods and walks off slowly. I watch him go, then turn back to Derrick. "You sure he's okay getting two plates?"

"He's fine. It's just right over there and it'll let him feel more independent. Besides, I had something else I wanted."

"Oh?" I ask, reading the low rumble in his voice. "What's that?"

"Like maybe I should have taken Jacob up on that cheerleader outfit offer," he whispers in my ear. "Minus the panties."

My throat goes dry, and I look into Derrick's eyes. "Behave yourself . . . and we'll see what happens when we get home. For now, though, I need a drink."

I get up and head to the back of the box, where Daniel is piling tortilla chips onto a big plate. "Here, let me help."

He looks over, then nods. "Is Derrick behaving himself?"

"As much as he normally does," I reply with a chuckle. "You know how he is."

"I do," he says, glancing back. "It's funny, but I guess he's always been meant for that show of his. He's always had a way with words, even when he was younger and wouldn't say much unless he really knew you. He's still a little old-fashioned, though, in some ways. Hopefully, that was my and his mom's doing. He just needed a very special woman to complete him. I'm glad he's found her now."

I blink, touched. "Thank you."

"You're welcome. I wish his mother could've been here to see it. Vanessa would have liked you a lot."

I look up, wiping at my eyes. *No raccoon eyes, no raccoon eyes* . . . "I wish I could've met her," I finally say, not trusting my emotions. "Let's get the rest of the grub, go enjoy the second half, and you can tell me what kind of woman she was."

---

*T*he rest of the game goes well, and it ends on a happy note as Jacob's team gets a close win. "Nice . . . home playoff game next week," Derrick says as we leave the stadium. "He'll enjoy that."

I smile, putting my arm around his waist. I don't know what exactly that means, but I loved being by Derrick's side and knowing that he's there for me just like I was there for him today. We've been tested, and though it wasn't pretty, we withstood the potential hellfire.

"You two go on, I'll be fine," Dad says when we reach the car. "I think after a game like that, I'm going to just go relax, and I'm sure for you two, the evening is just starting. I'll grab a taxi home and catch you later."

He flags down a taxi as if it were nothing, and we watch him get in, leaving Derrick and me holding each other in the chilly wind. "So . . . how was your first football game?"

I chuckle and hug him. "I enjoyed our little practice game more, but it was fun just being there with you guys. So what are we going to do?"

"I say we hit up Jacob's after party," he says. "I could use some adult supervision."

I laugh, and we get in his car, driving to a nearby nightclub. Walking in, I'm surprised to see a familiar face. "Elise?"

She looks like a million bucks in a sparkly, tight-fitting club dress, and when she turns around, a huge grin breaks across her face. "Hey, babe, why didn't you tell me you were coming?"

"Kind of spur of the moment . . . but what are you doing here?" I ask. Derrick gives a nod to Elise, but before he can say anything, someone calls his name from across the room and he turns. "Go," I tell him. "I'll catch up in a minute. Tell Jacob good game for me."

"I will," he says, kissing me on the cheek.

Derrick leaves with a wave, and Elise turns back to me. "So, what are you doing in town?" I ask as she leads me over to a table where another woman is sitting. "Hi."

"Hi," the woman, who honestly, I would never expect to be sitting with Elise, says. She immediately ignores me though, gushing to Elise. "Check it, babe! I was talking with some of the girls, and you'd never believe what Christian K is up to."

"What?" Elise asks, and I suddenly get it without her explaining. She's in town working. Guess a gossip columnist has to follow the gossip.

The woman looks over at me and smiles, then back at Elise. "You sure your friend here is up to hear about it?"

Elise sighs and grimaces. "With that, I'm not sure even *I* want to know," Elise says. "Why do the handsome ones have to be so fucked up?"

Her friend laughs, sipping at her drink. "Well, if you don't want to hear that, I've got an even better story to tell you."

The music's starting to heat up, and we have to lean in close to hear. "What?"

"You're never gonna believe it."

Elise grabs her drink, downing half of it in a single gulp. "Okay, I'm ready. Spill it!"

"Okay, well, check out across the room," the girl says, gesturing. "See him?"

I turn with Elise, seeing nothing until I recognize the guy at the bar. I almost missed it because his infamous hat is missing and the lights are landing on his bald head at all angles. "Is that?"

"Yep," the girl says. "Keith Perkins. You know, the country star?"

Elise hums, nodding. "The one who's been gathering the awards? What's he doing in a club like this?"

"Who knows? He seems to be going incognito without the hat, and maybe there's a little more to him than his public image says," gossip girl quips. "Anyway . . . watch him."

We do, and while I only see a man who's out having a good time, he seems to ignore all the women who hit on him, all of them beautiful. "Get my point?" the woman says.

Elise nods. "Yeah . . . players gon' play, but this one ain't playin' . . . interesting. Gotcha. Two more rounds on me."

"I think I'll go see Derrick," I whisper in Elise's ear. "I'll let you work, find your next scoop. Come see us with Jacob up in VIP when you get the chance?"

"You got it," Elise says, giving me a kiss on the cheek. "Have fun, babe. And congrats on the win."

I go find Derrick, who's toasting with Jacob. "To the future . . . well, I'm not gonna jinx you yet."

"Good, because I don't need any jinxing," Jacob says, chuckling. He clinks glasses with Derrick, then sees me. "Hey, Kat. Enjoy the game?"

"Had a ball," I quip. "But I think it's time to party."

And party we do. While we can't go overboard—Jacob's still got at least one more game and we have to drive home—we still enjoy ourselves. Jacob spends most of his time upstairs chatting with nearly every pretty woman who comes his way, but he's still gentlemanly with them.

I can see why Derrick likes him.

"Hey, wanna dance?" Derrick asks me as his ears perk up. "I love this song."

I nod my head, taking his hand and swaying with him down the stairs as the DJ plays a remix of Rhianna's *Only Girl*, and find a space on the dance floor. We're dressed nowhere near as fancy as some of the clubgoers, where undone buttons and high hemlines seem to be the norm . . . but I don't care as I sway with Derrick.

Turning around, I grind against him, humming happily as I feel something start to swell. "Is that for me?"

Derrick growls, lowering his lips to my ear. "I need you. Alone."

"Well," I reply, reaching back and cupping his cheek, "tell Jacob bye and let's get out of here."

The fresh air outside is brisk, but after the heat of the club, it's refreshing. Walking back to the car, we pass a park, stopping to take in the lights and the large, full moon that's peering down at us from over the trees. Suddenly, a fountain starts up, spraying into the air and underlit by deep red and blue lights like something out of a Disney movie. "Wow," I whisper, hugging against Derrick in the cold air, "it's beautiful."

"It is," Derrick agrees, hugging me tightly, his front pressing into my back. "Kat . . . thank you. For everything."

"Thank *you*," I reply softly, looking up to see him with a faraway look on his face. "Derrick? Penny for your thoughts?"

"Hmm?" he asks. I giggle and snuggle against him, feeling his still stiff cock at my back. "Mmm, this is such a romantic setup . . . you and me, alone, with the gorgeous fountain, but all I can think are dirty thoughts. I can't help it. That's what you do to me."

"Oh, really?" I ask, giggling a little. I look back into his eyes, which are glowing red and blue, reflecting the fountain's lights. "Tell me. I wanna hear every filthy thing."

Derrick lowers his voice to that sexy purr he knows drives me wild, a small smile dancing on his lips. "Like I want to get you back home, rip these clothes off you, and worship your body and fill your pussy so full you can't walk right tomorrow."

I grin, turning around and pressing my breasts against his body. "You want to fill my pussy so full of what . . . your long . . . thick . . . throbbing . . . cock?" I ask, drawing out the final word in that way that I know drives him crazy and reminds us both of just how far we've come. I reach down, running my hand over his bulging jeans, humming. "Seems that's exactly what you want to do."

Derrick gasps and nods. "Then let's go home. I think I owe you a nice, long massage tonight."

EPILOGUE

DERRICK

*T*he church looks beautiful, and the springtime air is warm, the scent of flowers wafting in from the trees outside. I feel a little cooped up in my suit, but that's okay. Today isn't about me.

It's not really about Kat either, although it's a very big deal for her. With her sister happily married and our own relationship being on track, today's sort of the capstone to her own circle of trust.

It's one more sign that fairy tales can happen. One night, after we made love, we lay in the dark and she explained a theory about happiness being an island in a sea of misery, comparing love to a small Styrofoam cup. I hadn't really understood the whole significance of her theory, but I promised to make our island the biggest, happiest one I could, and she smiled as she fell asleep in my arms. I decided that meant I was doing good. It's a growing process for us both.

Her whole life, she's been betrayed by every man whom she's ever given her heart to. And while I've not been perfect—I don't think any man is—the worst I've done over the past few months was forget to pick up Chinese takeout for dinner one night when she asked me to. Thankfully, the local spot down on the corner delivers in ten minutes flat.

Still, she's had a lifetime of insecurities and fears to get over, and we've conquered them together. I finally knew she was totally over it when she unpacked her last bag and turned in her key for her old place. No need to worry about a place to go or needing to leave because I've hurt her. Since then . . .

"Hey," Kat teases, looking so beautiful in her dress that I have a hard time taking my eyes off her. "You're daydreaming."

"Can you blame me?" I ask, taking in her peach-colored curves. We're in the back. There's still time before the ceremony starts, and I'm helping her with last-minute adjustments. "This sort of thing . . . let's face it, I get off on this sort of stuff."

Kat smiles and turns to snuggle against me. She's not perfect. She's flawed, and there are always going to be those little dark places in her heart. But they're fading day by day in the light of our love, pure and never-ending. "You big softie."

"Hey, I did my cardio last night," I tease with a wink. "At least, you didn't complain then."

Kat chuckles and hugs me tighter. "Okay, time to get ready. You're sitting up front, right?"

"Right," I reply, giving her another squeeze. "In fact, if I want that prime seat . . . tell your mom to have fun today. And tell Jess that you're a far hotter bridesmaid than she is."

Kat smiles and pats my chest. "Go on, no need to kiss my . . . well, not right now, at least."

I laugh and head into the sanctuary, settling into a seat in the second row on the bride's side. I've come to know most of Kat's family, and I'm sure I'd be accepted in the front row if I asked, but I guess I'm still sort of old-fashioned that way. Front row is for family only.

The church fills up, and when the music starts, I stand along with everyone else to turn and watch the procession. When Kat comes down the aisle, my mouth goes dry. She's so stunning, even though I just saw her earlier. The sunlight streams through the high stained glass window behind her, making her hair glow with inner health and beauty, truly my angel.

Watching her, the peach fades, replaced with white and lace, and I imagine her walking toward me. Yeah, according to stereotypes, women are supposed to be the ones who fantasize about weddings . . . but I'm fine being a romantic at heart. Maybe that's why I'm so good at being the Love Whisperer. In fact, that makes me more than fine with being romantic. I'm damn proud of it.

During the whole ceremony, I know that Kat's mom and

her man say things, but my eyes never leave Kat, even after Jessie catches me staring and smirks, elbowing her little sister.

At the reception, as soon as I can, I have Kat in my arms on the dance floor, swaying to a slow song from back in the day. I'm not downing it. Hell, I've played a little Vanessa Williams on *The Love Whisperer* from time to time myself

"You know . . . you're the most beautiful woman in the room," I tell her as we move to the music.

"Thank you," Kat replies. "Although you should occasionally blink. It'll help with those love goggles you've got on."

I laugh lightly and pull her in tight, lowering my voice intentionally, adding a little growl of gravel to the velvety smoothness so that it vibrates against her ear. "And that dress is something else. Makes me wonder what you've got on underneath it."

Kat casually shimmies in my arms, winking. "Is that a question? Remember that red set with the cami and boy shorts?"

My eyes glaze over as I think of that special set. Sure, we've bought other, sexier sets together, but that first set we played together with, the way I'd slipped the strap off her honeyed skin with my teeth . . . it's special. My cock thickens in my pants, and I nod softly.

Kat sees I'm in la-la land and chuckles. "Well, this dress is way too strappy and low-cut for that . . . or any bra at all.

But those boy shorts, the ones you love because they show the bottom curve on the outside of my cheeks and are so sheer you can see every bit of my pussy? I've got on those . . . and nothing else."

"Fuck, Kitty Kat," I groan, pulling her closer. "Every damn day, you know just how to drive me wild. Your mom and Bob had better cut the damn cake or I'm sneaking you out of here early for another peek and nibble of that delectable ass."

"Well, I suppose you could have some frosting . . . before your dessert," she purrs. "But I'm thinking the same thing as you."

Kat

"So everyone, that wraps up another evening. I'd like to thank everyone for joining me, Derrick King, for The Love Whisperer. I'll be taking a few days off, but don't worry, I've got plenty of stuff recorded for you. Tomorrow's show is a special episode on weddings: the good, the bad, the Bridezillas. So until I'm back, love yourself and each other. Goodnight."

The song starts, and I reach over, flicking off my radio and putting my stuff away. The office is almost totally deserted, but that's fine. I enjoy having these hours with just Derrick in my ear as I do my work. I guess going two for two on number one-rated apps across multiple platforms and another expected hit with our new game gets me a few extra benefits, and one of them is that I get to pick my own hours now . . . except for meetings.

I'm going to keep riding this for a while longer. I'm motivated, and taking a risk in doing another solo app after we wrap the game, but that's okay. A simple, easy to use standalone program that helps you lock down your devices and prevent spyware is something that's been in the PC market for a while, but it keeps being ignored in the mobile market. No longer, not when I'm done.

It's a high-profile project because while the inspiration came from our incident, the potential implementations could be amazing in securing governmental agency phones from tapping. I told Derrick that we could be the first beta-testers because since the big deal with Susannah, we haven't been as bold in phone conversations or FaceTime. We save our real dirty talk for the bedroom when it's just the two of us, with the phones in the other room. Still, we both miss the little thrill that comes from showing off for each other.

Getting behind the wheel of my car, I catch the end of the outro music for *The Love Whisperer*, then change the channel. The new show format has been awesome, simpler and more conversational with just Derrick. He's still got a producer. I talked with her once when I called in, but they decided to skip the co-host role and now the on-air is all Derrick.

People seem even more responsive now that they know he's happily in a relationship. It was rocky there at first when he lost the 'available' appeal, but people have come around, and he says it adds believability to his advice, even though he's always been pretty spot-on. According to Derrick, after the initial short-term dip, his ratings are stronger than ever. So much so that the bigwigs have been talking to him and Quincy about going the syndication route, and he even got invited to LA to be a guest panel member for some TV show. He hasn't decided about either opportunity yet though, saying he's happy with what he's got at work and at home.

I get home and change quickly, missing the sensation of having him here. We've both been working so hard the last few weeks, getting the programming just right on a difficult segment of coding, and Derrick's been tied up with recording his extra shows so he can do some extra project that he's been really secretive on. A few months ago, I would have been worried and distrustful . . . but that was then. Now, love and trust are together, and I've never doubted his intentions for a moment.

"Besides," I murmur as I quickly change clothes, "the good mornings and even better nights are that much sweeter when we spend every spare moment wrapped up in each other's arms, whispering dirty things in each other's ears."

I'm just slipping on my sexiest heels, not for height reasons but just because I know Derrick likes my legs in these, when he comes in from work. "Hey, babe. Good show. Loved the caller who wanted advice on self toys."

Derrick comes over and gives me a kiss on the cheek, hugging me from behind. "Thanks," he growls, nibbling at my ear and sending tingles down my spine. "Fuck, you're so damn gorgeous, Kitty Kat. Those heels make me want to bend you over and lick down the line of your legs before flipping you onto your back and making them become 'in the air' shoes.

I raise an eyebrow, moaning lightly as he licks at the curve of my earlobe and traces a single fingertip along my upper thigh. "Why aren't we doing that, then? Let's stay home, order in, and change into something more . . . comfortable while you get a taste of my pussy and I get a sip of *your* cream. Then we can eat to regain our strength and fuck again . . . all night long."

Derrick moans and kisses my neck again before releasing me and stepping back. "I wanted to do this differently, more . . . something, but I can't wait anymore."

Reaching into his jacket, Derrick takes out a plain black jewelry box. It's narrow, but I don't care about the box . . . I care about the look in his eyes and the love in his heart as he opens the box to reveal a beautiful diamond ring. It's not gaudy. It's classic, a simple platinum band with a single square-cut diamond in the middle. "Derrick . . ."

He takes my hand, kissing my knuckles softly. "Kat, you thought you didn't deserve a fairytale, that it was rare. And while it's true it is rare, you most definitely deserve the happily ever after, and I hope that you'll choose to spend it with me, as my wife."

There's no other answer I can give except a choked nod and a small squeal of excitement. "Yes . . . with all my heart, yes."

Derrick slips the ring on my finger before sweeping me up in his arms, spinning me around. "That's my Kitty Kat. Thank you for giving me my dream."

I hug him tightly, kissing his lips hard. "No, thank you. Thank you for showing me that I didn't need a fairytale fantasy. What I needed was real love from a real man. After that, the dream will happen on its own."

Our kiss deepens, my silky dress letting me slide down Derrick's body as our joy quickly mixes with intense heat. I can feel his cock already hardening for me, and my nipples are stiff and electric against the slick fabric. Getting on my knees, I look up at him. "Now, I think I want to start our celebration. You can call the delivery guy while I have a suck of your big—"

"Don't say it . . . unless you want me to be too distracted to order," Derrick chuckles. "Mmm . . . sexy, smart, loving, mine, and oh, so dirty in a good way. My Kitty Kat."

I reach for his waistband, undoing his belt while I grin. "I want General Tso's chicken. And as for your being distracted . . . well, just think—after our food, you can bend me over the couch and fuck me any way you want. But first, I'm going to enjoy a taste of this amazing cock."

I draw the word out the way I always do for him, knowing that it's driven him crazy since day one, still does today, and hopefully will for many more happy years of dirty talk.

His cock pops free, and I look up at him. He grins down at me, telling me what he knows I want to hear. "Go on, Kitty Kat. Suck my cock down your pretty little throat like my naughty girl."

My mouth waters, and I immediately swallow him whole. Dirty? Maybe, but nothing could be better.

We'll have to call the family to tell them the news . . . later.

Thank you for reading. Continue for the bonus read, Motorhead, Book 7 in the Irresistible Bachelor Series. However each book is a different couple and can be read on its own.

DIRTY LAUNDRY: COMING SOON!

*E*ach book in the "Get Dirty" series will be a different couple. Here is a special sneak peek at the cover Dirty Laundry, book 2! It'll hopefully give you clues as to who the next book is about. Join my reader group and let me know who you think it is!

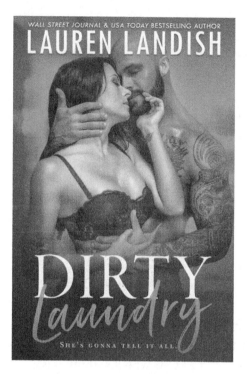

Coming Late Feb.

Join my mailing list (www.laurenlandish.com) and receive 2 FREE ebooks! You'll also be the first to know of new releases, sales, and giveaways. If you're on Facebook, come join my Reader Group!

ABOUT THE AUTHOR

Join Landish Landish, my Facebook Reader Group!

Connect with Lauren Landish

www.laurenlandish.com
admin@laurenlandish.com

Made in the USA
Middletown, DE
14 April 2022

64270188R00169